A Titanic Disaster

Mercer felt slightly ridiculous. Not only was he "new boy", but as ship's Medical Officer he was regarded by the crew with something less than respect. He might be a fully qualified medico but his qualifications were required by space travel regulations. He was definitely not a professional spaceman—and therefore, to the other officers, simply an added burden to be coped with in the daily routine of a perfectly safe ship.

Until disaster struck.

Then suddenly Mercer's inexperience was equalled by that of everyone else aboard. The crew knew what to do with the ship—and they were very busy with it indeed.

The passengers, in their pathetic, plastic pods, unprepared and completely helpless, were entirely Doctor Mercer's problem . . .

LIFEBOAT

James White

A Del Rey Book

BALLANTINE BOOKS • NEW YORK

A Del Rey Book
Published by Ballantine Books

ISBN 0-345-28693-6

Manufactured in the United States of America

First Edition: September 1972
Second Printing: March 1980

First Canadian Printing: October 1972

Cover art by John Berkey

Chapter 1

The departure lounge was half full since the coach had left on its first trip to the ship, but it had not grown any quieter. Excitement, impatience and natural anxiety had combined to raise the noise level of every conversation until the background music and its intended soothing effect were obliterated. Ignoring the low and sinfully soft couches scattered around the large, cool room, the remaining passengers for *Eurydice* clustered about the exit ramp like jet travelers bucking for a seat by a window.

None of them were watching Mercer directly. Relieved, he dropped his eyes to the papers which he had not been studying for the past half hour and wondered if replacing them in his briefcase would be a signal for passengers to come surging over to introduce themselves or ask questions. He already knew all of their names, having memorized the passenger list, since his job would consist largely of looking after them. But right now they were still strangers—for the simple reason that he did not know which face went with any given name. He decided to savor his last remaining moments of introversion before he had to join the ship.

Mercer had no sooner made this decision and was beginning to feel pleasantly guilty about it when a pair of small feet moved into the area of floor covered by his downcast eyes and stopped a few yards in front of his chair. He looked up slowly.

Black sneakers, black slacks, black tunic and long-visored cap, which carried an improbable quantity of insignia and plastic scrambled eggs. The uniform had probably been a good fit last Christmas, but now it was a little short and tight. Even though the body over-filling the uniform was sturdy and well-nourished, the face had the pinched, big-eyed look of the over-imaginative, intelligent and probably highly nervous type. Mercer did not have to read the identity patch on his chest to know that this was Robert Mathewson, because there was only one ten-year-old boy on the passenger list.

They stared at each other for a long time, with Mercer feeling as tongue-tied as the boy looked. This was ridiculous, he told himself irritably as the silence began to drag and both their faces shifted deeper into the infrared. This was, after all, his first social contact with a passenger, and one this young should be easy— good practice for him, in fact.

Clearing his throat, he said, "I didn't know that we had been assigned a cadet for this trip, but I can certainly use your help—"

"Bobby, I told you not to wander off!" said a voice from behind him. It was a feminine, harassed voice, belonging, Mercer saw as he turned, to the boy's mother. She was very young, dark-haired and with a face subtly distorted by tension and worry, so that he could not decide whether it was pretty or downright lovely. She rushed on, "You were told not to talk to strangers and that means not making a nuisance of yourself to the ship's officers. I'm sorry about this, sir. You're obviously busy and he knows better than to . . ."

"It's quite all right, m'am," began Mercer, but already she was dragging her son towards the largest group of passengers, still scolding and apologizing and not listening to him at all.

For a few minutes he watched the boy in the space officer's outfit and his mother in the issue coveralls which the passengers wore shipside. The one-piece coverall was not exactly shapeless—especially not in Mrs. Mathewson's case—but it obeyed the dictates of the current neo-puritan fashion which insisted on covering the female form on public occasions from neck to ankles.

Suddenly restless, Mercer stuffed the papers back into his briefcase and stood up. He began pacing slowly around the empty end of the lounge, staring at the large, full-color pictures which were closely spaced along the walls so that he would not have to look at, and perhaps become involved with, the passengers. His first contact with two of them had not exactly helped his self-confidence.

Like the background music, the pictures were designed to be reassuring—there was only one take-off, a few interior shots, and the rest showed *Eurydice* or her sister ships coming in to land beneath enormous, brightly-colored dirigible parachutes, or floating in the ten-miles-distant landing lake and held upright by a collar of inflated life pods while the passengers slid laughing down a transparent tube into a waiting boat. The pictures stressed the Happy Return rather than the Voyage itself, Mercer thought cynically as he moved to the big periscopic window which looked out over the field.

Two miles away, *Eurydice* stood by her gantry, clean but for the passenger boarding bridge. Only the topmost hundred feet or so of the ship proper, comprising the controlroom, crew quarters and the upper members of the structure which supported the rotating section, was visible. The service and life-support modules, water tank, and nuclear power unit were wrapped in thick swathes of boosters. A mile farther down the line stood the empty gantry which had serviced *Minerva* before her departure four months earlier, and beyond that, rippling faintly in the heat, there rose a ship identical to *Eurydice* except for its much larger and more complex wrapping of boosters.

Nobody talked about that particular ship, and it did

not have a name. Like the homecoming pictures scattered around the lounge, it was meant to be a reassuring sight, but somehow it was nothing of the kind.

The only difference between the passengers and himself, Mercer thought sourly, was that he had nobody to talk loudly and nervously *to . . .*

"*Eurydice,* sir?"

He turned to find a hostess standing behind him. She was wearing one of the old-style mirror plastic uniforms—described as pseudo-futuristic by female fashion writers and with animal growls of appreciation by men regardless of occupation—and for the first few seconds that was all he saw. He was vaguely aware of glittering boots, a hat streamlined for Mach Three and short cloak thrown back over shoulders that were a flawless, creamy pink, and intensely aware of the rest of the get-up, which was virtually topless and well-nigh bottomless. When he finally raised his eyes, Mercer discovered that she was not just a beautiful body—she had a nice face, too.

"The coach is waiting, sir," she said. Her smile was polite and not at all impatient, and her eyes were laughing at him.

Mercer nodded and began walking briskly towards the exit, where the passengers were already climbing the ramp which led from the cool, blast-proof lounge to the blistering heat of the surface one hundred feet above. She hurried to keep pace with him, and Mercer wondered why until he realized suddenly that they were, after all, fellow workers, servants of the same company, colleagues. The realization made it possible for him to untie his suddenly knotted tongue.

"I'm sorry if I appeared rude back there," he said, trying hard to keep his eyes on a level with her face, "but it seems to me that, to anyone leaving Earth perhaps never to return, you make a very nice last impression. In fact, if there was a little more time before take-off it would not take much to convince me not to leave at all. Or come to think of it, when I get back in eight months we could meet and maybe—"

"What you are thinking would probably get us both into trouble, with my husband," she broke in, laughing. "This is your first trip, sir."

It was a statement with not the slightest suggestion of a question mark tacked onto the end. Trying to hide his irritation, Mercer said, "I didn't think it showed."

She was silent while they left the lounge and began to mount the flat spiral ramp leading to the surface. The radiation doors which interrupted the ascending tunnel every twenty yards had been dogged open, so that the hot, dusty air from above was already reaching them. When she spoke, the last of the passengers were out of sight and hearing, hidden by the curve of the tunnel and their own self-generated wall of sound.

"It shows, sir," she said seriously, "but I'm learning caution in my old age. You see, I don't seem to be able to give advice without also giving offence, and so unless I'm asked . . ."

"I'm asking," said Mercer dryly.

She nodded and went on. "You are the tall, hungry-looking type who suits that black rig—but you, especially, must be careful how you wear it. That rakish angle of the hat is wrong for *Eurydice,* and some of your pocket zips are done and some half-done—you haven't got that right, either, and at this stage of the game you shouldn't even try. Even the plays which you've been watching so carefully on TV never get it right, so don't feel too bad about it.

"This mystique with the zips and caps which veteran spacemen practice," she went on, "began as sheer sloppiness, no doubt, but now the so-and-sos change the rules after every trip just to confuse people. But you, sir, are not yet a veteran, so it is much better that you don't get it at all than get it wrong. In any case, there are two officers on every ship who do not subscribe to these little idiosyncrasies of dress. They are the Captain, who is too important to care about such things, and the other is you, sir, who is generally considered to be the lowest form of life in the service and who is not supposed to get ideas above his station. But you know all this already, I hope."

She was watching him intently, but she relaxed when he smiled and said, "I was told, but not precisely in those words. The general idea seems to be that since our passengers have to be physically fit to be allowed to make the trip in the first place, my medical know-how is not essential, and since I have no other special-ized technical training useful in space, my duties will be largely those of a steward. The responsibility for ensuring that the customers have a happy and con-fortable trip is mine, apparently, and up until now, I'm sorry to say, the thought of mixing with and looking after more than forty healthy people has me scared stiff—"

"You are being too negative, sir," she broke in sharply. "You may be little more than the ship's stew-ard, but you must not act like one or even think like one. And you apologized to me twice during, oh, five minutes of conversation. That's bad. You must be the strong, silent type if you want to gain the respect of your charges. Failing that, you can be the weak, silent type—just so long as you're silent, reserved, some-what aloof at all times and never tell them your trou-bles. Remember that the passengers don't know that you are just a glorified steward, and they must never suspect that you are their servant or your first trip will be hell, and your last so far as *Eurydice* is concerned. Because if even once you have to go to the real officers with a passenger problem, your name is mud, and you'll never—"

She was beginning to sound rather emotional, Mercer thought. He held up his hand and said, "What did *I* ever do to you?"

She was quiet for the next dozen paces, then she

laughed and said, "Not a thing. But you can return my favor if you like. I would like to have a few extra minutes on board. If I could stay up there with the first group of passengers while you took up the second batch, I really would appreciate that, sir."

Return what favor? Mercer wondered, then thought that her advice and criticism had been just that, even if it had nearly lifted the skin off his back. He nodded.

"Oh, *thank* you, sir."

Definitely the emotional type, he thought.

A few minutes later they reached the upper end of the ramp and stood blinking in the twin glare of the afternoon sun and the mirror-bright coach. His dark uniform soaked up the heat like a thermal sponge, and beside him the girl became a glittering, truncated cone as she pulled the cloak around her shoulders.

"Sorry to spoil your view," she said, "but I don't tan in the sun, I frizzle up. You take the seat beside mine at the rear—you'll have more leg-room—and ignore the flashing lights on my call panel. People always sit on the arm-rest buttons while finding a seat. Be with you in a minute, sir."

By the time she rejoined him he had used the cosmetic mirror set into her service panel to adjust his cap, which was now absolutely straight and as level as the distant blue line of the landing lake. He had already checked his zips. The coach was already picking up speed towards *Eurydice's* gantry and the noise level was keeping pace with it. Two seats in front of them a man was complaining bitterly because the coaches weren't big enough to move everyone to the ship at the same time, another was insisting that at the price this trip was costing his company he was damn well going to watch the take-off from a port, and from farther along the coach two different call lights were blinking.

"It's high time," said Mercer, rising, "that I started getting to know my patients—I mean passengers."

Her small, strong hand pushed him back into the seat.

"I'll handle it," she said. "Until they are all trussed up and safe in their acceleration couches they are my responsibility. Sit there, and save your strength."

Chapter II

Because it was a widely accepted fact that many people could undertake plane trips and even interplanetary voyages without qualms and yet be scared silly by three hundred feet of altitude, the elevator which took *Eurydice's* passengers up to the main entry lock was completely enclosed. But that low-ceilinged, windowless cage had a very subduing effect, Mercer noted. It was as if the passengers realized that they were taking their first tiny step spacewards and that there was still time to step back. Or was he simply putting thoughts into the passengers' minds because the same thoughts were going through his own?

The cage was uncomfortably crowded, but the passengers were somehow managing to keep their distance from each other, and they did not even look at him. Starting to introduce himself in these conditions was impossible—he would simply make himself look and sound ridiculous. But he could at least nod at young Mathewson without loss of dignity or doing irreparable harm to his image.

But the boy tried to salute him and jabbed a passenger in the stomach with his elbow, his mother grabbed his arm and began apologizing all round, and Mercer retreated behind his personal wall of silence wondering, as they reached the top and the passengers preceded him into the ship, if it was possible to project an image so strong and silent that he would not have to speak to anyone at all for the entire four months of the trip.

First Officer Prescott was waiting for him just inside the outer seal. He ran his eyes quickly from Mercer's cap to his sneakers and back again, looking faintly surprised, but when he spoke he sounded more than faintly disappointed. "I thought you weren't going to make it. What kept you?"

"I was told to come aboard with the last coachload of passengers. . . ." began Mercer. But Prescott was obviously not listening, so he concentrated on being strong and silent again as he passed into the lock antechamber. He could feel his face burning, so the chances were that he was fooling nobody but himself.

The Captain was standing just inside the seal, looking cool, correct, and with his features, if anything, stiffer than his too-erect body. He was looking through Mercer and the double hull behind him at some remembered object or event which claimed all of his attention.

He had met Collingwood and the other officers very briefly during his training, and the Captain had been the only ship's officer who had not made him feel like crawling under the nearest stone. But now it looked as if Collingwood was angry about something, probably the misdemeanor of the girl deserting half a coachload of passengers. Perhaps one of them had actually complained to him about it, and now she was standing beside the Captain looking as if she was about to cry.

Mercer felt sorry for her. She was very easy to like and even easier to feel sorry for, and in a way he was responsible for her trouble because he had agreed to her request. He wanted badly to apologize but remembered that she did not like people who apologized too often. He stopped. The Captain was still staring into the middle distance, not even seeing him.

"Good-bye, m'am," he said.

It came close to being the shortest and most uninspired farewell of all time, but her reaction literally rocked him back on his heels.

"Take care of yourself," she said, standing on tiptoe and giving him a very warm but sisterly kiss on the cheek. Then she looked at him very seriously and added, "Take care of all of them, sir."

Mercer had instinctively put his arms around her waist, both to keep his balance and because it seemed to be the thing to do, then let them drop to his sides. She had not, he saw, committed some trifling misdemeanor and been told off for it—there was far too much tension and sheer misery in her expression. He wondered what kind of trouble could make a girl with a disposition like hers react like this, and if he could help. But today he seemed to have left his inspiration in his other suit, and all he could manage was a sickly smile and a line of dialogue which was too trite for words.

"What about your husband, m'am?"

"He doesn't mind," said the Captain, "provided you two don't make a habit of it." Suddenly he laughed, and the girl began laughing too—the way people did who were trying hard not to cry. She turned from Mercer to hang a stranglehold on the Captain's neck. The kiss she gave him was anything but sisterly.

Mercer was still staring at them when Prescott's finger dented his shoulder. "Are you some kind of voyeur, Mercer? We have work to do upstairs."

"Yes, sir."

But when they had climbed to the passenger level Prescott paused for a few moments before continuing towards the control deck. Pitching his voice low because of the passengers lying all around them, he said, "They're all yours, Mercer. Keep them quiet and comfortable and don't let anyone be sick outside of his plastic bag—that is funny only on television. If you should have a problem, hesitate before calling on me for help—hesitate for as long as possible because we will be very busy and will not take kindly to doing your job for you. Understood?"

"Yes, sir."

Prescott shook his head. "You have made a great start to your first voyage, Mercer, and I shudder to think of what you might do before it ends. I mean, practically making love to the Captain's wife before his very eyes—"

"At the risk of sounding a cad, sir," said Mercer, "she started it."

"And another thing, Mercer. We do not salute or click heels or call anyone 'sir' except the Captain, and he does not insist on it. Invisible discipline is what we aim for, and an air of relaxed informality— well, informality anyway. Just look after your passengers without getting too close to any of them and keep out of the way of the ship's officers—"

"It looks as if I'll have a very lonely trip, Mr. Prescott," said Mercer quietly, but he was unable to keep the anger from showing in his tone.

"In my experience," Prescott replied in a voice that was sarcastic rather than actively hostile, "people like you take a trip like this as a means to an end. In your profession, space experience automatically puts you at the head of the queue where the juiciest research appointments are concerned, and even in private practice it is enough to allow you to triple your fees. Perhaps we will be lucky; you will stay out of trouble with the passengers, keep yourself to yourself and spend your free time in your cabin studying some of those books you brought along."

"You'll be lucky."

Prescott ignored both the anger and the ambiguity in Mercer's reply. He said, "I hope so. But you are going to have company in a moment and I haven't time to chat, even to overexposed ministering angels. See you."

Mercer turned as the First Officer continued his climb to the cone. The two hostesses who had been checking and strapping in the passengers on arrival were just a little overexposed, and neither could hold a candle to Mrs. Captain. Or maybe it was just that his artistic appreciation had been deadened by the recent exchange with Prescott. He nodded, uncomfortably aware that his face was still red.

"The passengers are settled in, sir," said the dark-haired one. "All have been given medication, but you might keep an eye on Mr. Saddler and Mr. Stone, who may be trying to prove something—I think they palmed their capsules."

Mercer nodded without speaking.

"Don't let him bother you, sir," said the blonde one, reading his expression if not his mind. "He is an exceptionally good officer, believe it or not, even if he does lack charm."

"Surely," said Mercer, "you aren't his mother?"

The girl laughed. "No, and nobody said they *loved* him. But we have to go now and separate the Collingwoods—they swing in the boarding gantry in five minutes. Good luck, sir."

"And good hunting," added the other.

When they had gone Mercer stood for a moment looking slowly around the passenger deck, feeling lonely despite being knee-deep and surrounded within a wall to wall carpet of people, most of whom were staring at him. This is just like the simulator, he told himself firmly, complete with ship noises, muted countdown from the wall speakers, the paint and plastic smell of the acceleration couches, and the pressure of cool, artificially fresh air on his face—exactly the same, except that the couches were not being occupied by bored junior clerks from the administration building next door and the sounds and smells were real.

His job now was to give real comfort and reassurance to his charges, not just the simulated kind.

According to the instruction book and the psychologist who had taken him through it, it was a simple job. At this stage the passengers were already wrapped in broad acceleration webbing; even the shape of the couches was reminiscent of a cradle, and the calm, competent figure of a ship's officer moving among them was a father-figure tucking them in for the night. Greeting them individually by name, making a perfunctory check on the tightness of their straps, asking if they were comfortable, and dealing, very briefly, with any special problems they might have was all that was necessary to reassure them at this time.

At this time, his psychologist-instructor had added drily, he had over forty people to process pre-flightwise and less than sixty minutes to do it in, so there was just not the time to undertake deep analysis.

Surprisingly, it *was* simple.

The couches were laid out parallel and with the passengers' heads pointing in the same direction so that they could all watch the large projection screen set on the underside of the deck above. The walking space between them was about six inches wide, except where the curvature of the inner hull allowed more. He knelt briefly beside each couch, reading the passengers' name tags as he checked their straps, saying the prescribed words, and keeping an eye on the time by not looking at his watch in the same way that he did not seem to be looking at the name tags stitched to their coveralls when he spoke to them. He had to give the impression of being calm, unhurried, and concerned with their individual welfare, the book said, and theoretically he could take all the time he needed to ensure his passengers' comfort before takeoff. This was a passenger ship, after all, and a problem with one or more of the passengers was the only acceptable reason short of a serious malfunction for calling a Hold.

But Mercer would have to have a very strong reason for holding or the launch-control people would have caustic things to say, the Captain would probably go critical, and Prescott, who seemed to be a pretty poisonous character at the best of times, would certainly make his life miserable for the rest of the voyage.

"Are you comfortable, Mr. Saddler?" Mercer said pleasantly to the next in line; then he stopped. This was one of the tough guys who had not taken his medication. Mercer stared at the man's face without really seeing it while his mind sought in vain for a pleasant and friendly way of telling him to take his anti-nausea pill and not be a fool. By the end of the allotted minute Mercer still did not have the answer, and he saw that the passenger's face was becoming apprehensive and that he was refusing to meet Mercer's eyes. Suddenly he wriggled sideways in his straps so that he could reach his breast pocket.

"I'm sorry," he mumbled, "I nearly forgot to take my pill."

"It can happen," said Mercer pleasantly, "in the excitement."

The next two couches were occupied by the Mathewsons. Judging by the glazed look in her eyes, one of the hostesses had seen fit to slip Mrs. Mathewson a small-calibre sleep bomb which was already taking effect. Perhaps she had been frightened. Her son's eyes were enormous, but not with fear. Mercer found himself envying the hot, bright, uncomplicated excitement of the boy. With Mercer there was very little that happened for the first time. When it did happen for the first time, as it would in a very few minutes from now, the sensation would be diluted and deadened by the emotional impurities of fear and guilt; and by his maturity and intelligence, which would insist on computing his chances of meeting disaster during the period of maximum stress that was takeoff; and by the other excitements of his short adult life, which had reduced his capacity to respond to this one. He wondered suddenly if the real reason for his being here was the fear that if he had stayed put he would have used up Earth and everything it had to offer and joined everyone else in the desperate search for small variations on old sensations.

Mercer smiled. Compared with the life most of his

friends had led, his had been almost monastic. Below him, Bobby Mathewson smiled back.

The next couch was empty, for the very good reason that it was his own. Beyond it was the one belonging to Stone, the other passenger suspected of missing out on his pre-takeoff medication. Mercer tried the blank stare on him that had worked so well with Saddler, hoping that the man's guilty conscience would do the rest, but Stone simply stared back at him. Maybe his conscience was clear. Mercer had to be content with clearing his throat loudly and slipping a plastic bag between the other's chest straps where Stone could reach it quickly.

They would be different people in space, he thought as he gave a careful last look around. Different but not necessarily better. The book had gone into great detail regarding the odd quirks and outright personality changes—naturally occurring, of course, not those induced by drugs—which some people developed during space voyage. It went into even greater detail about the deep-rooted psychological reasons for it. Mercer sighed, lay down on his couch, and swallowed his own anti-nausea medication while he was strapping in.

On the screen above him the picture of *Eurydice* and the gantry was replaced by a view of the distant hills and landing lake as someone switched to the on-board TV camera. He slipped on his headset and said, "Mercer. Passenger section ready."

Collingwood's voice sounded in his earpiece. "So I see. But are you quite sure that they are all settled and medicated? I realize that you are keen and are probably trying to impress me with your efficiency, but I shall not be impressed if a lot of passengers try to turn themselves inside out while we are dumping the boosters."

The tone softened a little as he went on. "Missing the pip is an inconvenience these days instead of a disaster. Our launch window is as wide as we want to make it, so if there is anything worrying you that might require a Hold, let's have it, Mercer."

While the Captain had been talking, Mercer had been thinking about Stone and wondering how he could explain his suspicions without sounding like a fussy old woman. He couldn't.

"No problems, sir."

"Good. We lift in four minutes."

Mercer spent the time checking that the vacuum cleaner under his couch was handy and worrying about the period of weightless maneuvering which would begin when they went into Earth orbit. Both the book and his instructor had painted awful pictures of weightless nausea running wild. It could become critical, they had said, a chain reaction which could spread even to those who had taken medication, and the job of clearing the air was difficult and distasteful. An incident like that was the one thing guaranteed to sour the whole voyage.

He was still worrying when the boosters ignited and acceleration piled invisible weights on his chest. The projection screen showed the launch complex and landing lake shrinking below them. More and more territory crawled in from the edges of the screen: the pale cross-hatching of a town, the grey smears of mountains flattened by the near-vertical sunlight, tiny layers of shadow sandwiched between the ground and the clouds. He moved his head carefully so as to watch Stone.

Anyone with a TV in their living room had seen it all before.

Chapter III

"This is the Captain, ladies and gentlemen. I hope that you are comfortable and that you will have a pleasant trip. We shall make two complete orbits of Earth, during which a number of minor course-corrections will be necessary for us to match orbits with Station Three to dump our boosters. Please remain strapped in until these maneuvers are completed, which will be in a little under four hours after we reach the vicinity of the station.

"During the next fifteen minutes you will notice periodic fogging of the picture of Earth's face being projected on your screen," he went on quietly. "This is in all respects normal and is caused by the venting of surplus fuel from the boosters prior to their delivery at Station Three. Thank you."

"Roughly translated," Prescott's voice continued in Mercer's ear-plug, "nothing out of the ordinary is happening except that we are slightly off course due to us taking off exactly on time. Nobody bothers to do that these days and launch control don't have to be all that accurate, either. In the old days this sort of thing would have been very serious. But now, with virtually unlimited reaction mass—"

"Careful, Bob," broke in the Captain's voice, "or you'll be lecturing again."

"Nobody listens," said Prescott shortly, then went on: "As a result we shall be using booster steering power at increasingly frequent intervals as we approach Three. During the final thirty minutes, Mercer, keep a sharp eye on your passengers."

"Will do," said Mercer, then added: "In the meantime we will be weightless practically all of the time, as I understand it. Have I permission to rig the cabin dividers?"

"Yes," said Prescott.

Mercer lay unmoving for perhaps a minute, thinking about Prescott and the Captain. The First Officer, who was not a pleasant personality to begin with, was being actively unpleasant towards him, probably to remind him firmly and continuously that he was a space officer in name only. In complete contrast was the Captain, who was patient and considerate and, so far as Mercer could see, pleasant to everyone including Prescott. He wondered if the other crew-members would emulate Prescott or the Captain in their behavior towards him, or if it would fall somewhere in between. He supposed that it would depend on how they had been raised to think of second-class citizens.

But suppose Prescott's feelings towards him were shared by the others—even by the Captain—and the only difference was that the first officer's reactions were honest while those of the others were cloaked, for the moment, by surface kindliness and consideration.

Mercer shook his head angrily, trying to derail this highly uncomfortable train of thought. Surely he could take a little unpleasantness for the duration of the trip. Large numbers of people on Earth were made to feel inferior for each and every day of their lives. But he still felt like telling Prescott what he could do simply to relieve his feelings, and suddenly there was something he could tell the First Officer to do. He thumbed the transmit switch.

"Mercer. Our TV picture of the surface is cork-screwing as well as fogging. Too much of that might make our passengers feel uncomfortable. Can you—"

The screen went blank and Prescott said, "Right. Do you want to show a film instead?"

"I don't think so," Mercer replied. "Watching me trying to tie down the cabin dividers should be entertainment enough."

Before releasing his harness he waited to see if Prescott would have the last, unpleasant word, then decided that Collingwood had probably told the First Officer to go easy on the new man.

The main supports for the cabins were two tough plastic rings just over half the interior diameter of the passenger module. Together with the four main support ropes and the inner spacer lines which kept the rings apart, the rings were clipped at intervals of a few feet to the underside of the deck above, so as to keep the cordage from coming adrift during acceleration. Mercer pulled himself around the anchored rings, releasing the fastenings and tossing the main supporting ropes very gently towards the deck below—all except the last one, the end of which he wrapped around his hand. Turning head downwards, he sighted himself at the rope's lashing point between two couches and, with all eyes upon him, kicked out hard.

In theory, the mass and momentum of his body would draw out the double rings, whose inertia would slow him to a stop before he actually hit the deck. But Mercer, who had practiced this operation in a ground simulator with a system of weights duplicating the effect of weightlessness, had been sure that if he kicked too hard he would crack his skull on the deck or, if his aim was bad, bury it in someone's stomach. As a result he was a little too cautious; he did not succeed in pulling both rings far enough from their housing. Instead of reaching the deck, his misjudged dive stopped a few feet above the acceleration couches, and he began to swing towards the middle of the compartment.

Ignoring the grins as well as the eyes watching him,

he cleared his throat and said, "Would one of you mind grabbing my feet?"

Immediately the deck sprouted a forest of clutching hands, which eventually succeeded in checking his swing. But the rings had begun to swing as well, giving him a lot more slack on the support rope he was holding, so that he toppled slowly and very gently across two doubly-upholstered couches, the upper layers in both cases being female. The layer called Miss Mac-Roberts giggled, and the other, whose name he could not read because of the topological features distorting her identity patch, said "Pleased to meet you."

Mercer apologized gravely and began moving back to the lashing point by gripping the edges of intervening couches with his free hand and pulling himself along. Within a few minutes he had the support rope in position and pulled taut.

Above him the two rings swung and vibrated slowly, shaking their attached cordage into the beginnings of a weightless tangle. Mercer dived carefully across the deck, snatched the second support rope out of the air as he passed it, and checked himself with the other hand against the couch beside its lashing point. He was beginning to get the hang of it.

By the time the first surge of steering thrust came he had the supporting lines in position and was beginning to weave a double web of cabin dividers between the now-rigid rings and the inner skin of the hull. His ear-piece had bleeped a five-second acceleration warning, so he had plenty of time to wedge himself between two couches and hold on. But when it came the surge was so gentle and his grip on the couch edges so tight that he felt ridiculous. When a double bleep signaled the cessation of thrust he nodded silently to the passengers on each side of him and returned to work.

During the next three hours the surges came with increasing frequency, but he was usually close enough to a bulkhead or one of the rings to hold on until they had passed—although on one occasion he mis-judged, ending the weightless tumble which followed with an awkward handstand on the edges of someone's couch so as to avoid butting them in the stomach.

It was not easy to maintain a pleasantly grave expression or to pretend that this sort of activity was in all respects normal as he murmured "Sorry, m'am" and returned, like an industrious, if ungainly, spider, to weave his web.

Looking incredibly fragile and completely purpose-less, his double web neared completion despite these interruptions. In its sub-orbital configuration during the initial, powered stage of their trip, the thing was simply a highly porous obstruction to anyone wanting to watch the screen. But when the reactor, which would give them a half-G of thrust for the first two days of the flight, closed down, artificial gravity would be supplied by spinning the passenger section about the longitudinal axis of the ship. The walls of the inner hull would then become the floor and the double web would support clip-on plastic sheets, and the passengers would have cabins and privacy of a sort.

The cabins would even be roofed over, so that crew members moving along the weightless axis between con-trol and the power module aft would not be able to see the sort of things that were reputed to go on in passenger-carrying spaceships.

People tended to forget the rules when they were far from home, his instructor had warned him, and the degree of forgetfulness was in direct proportion to the distance.

His mind was not entirely on his job, he realized suddenly, or he would not have missed hearing the thrust warning. As it was, he found the section of support ring he was working on moving away from him, and he instinctively tightened his grip on the attached line he was holding.

Just as the line was drawing taut against its ring, thrust was applied at right angles to the previous surge and he began a slow swing around the support ring, a swing which would ultimately wrap his line tightly around the ring. For a few seconds this did not worry him, but then he realized that as the line wound itself tight it would shorten and his speed of rotation would increase—it was speeding up already, in fact. With his free hand he reached for one of the divider ropes as it whirled past, but could only touch it. All he succeeded in doing was to start himself spinning on the end of his rope as well as describing diminishing circles around the ring.

Dizzy and confused, Mercer tried to work out how fast he would be traveling by the time his line was completely wound around the ring. Almost certainly it would be too fast for him to transfer his grip from the rope to the ring, and if he let go at that speed he would go bulleting into the deck, bulkheads, or passengers like a stone from a slingshot. The time to let go was *now,* while he was still moving relatively slowly. But his hand seemed to have a mind of its own —the more he thought of letting go the stronger became its grip on the rope.

Mercer closed his eyes and tried to think. He had more than two feet of slack wrapped around his hand; if he released that, then the radius of his swing would be increased and his rotation slowed. He would do just that, and hold on to the last few inches of rope until he was swinging towards the inner hull wall, then bend his knee to absorb the shock of landing and let go.

But the end of the rope slipped from his hand before he was ready, and he went rumbling slowly toward the center of the deck. For a moment he thought that he would be fantastically lucky and land on his own couch, but instead he landed sprawling on the one beside it.

The passengers began to applaud, and Mrs. Mathewson said crossly, "Do you always try to land on defenseless women?"

"Only the pretty ones, m'am," Mercer said before

he realized that his great relief at not breaking his neck was possibly not shared by the passenger he had landed on. But before he could apologize properly his earpiece bleeped a thrust warning and he squirmed into his own couch.

He had the webbing around his ankles when thrust tilted him gently to one side, then the other, then tried to lift him out of the couch and twist him at the same time. Someone grunted and gave an odd-sounding cough. Mercer swung around to see the passenger called Stone rapidly filling his plastic bag.

Stone had been a little late in getting the bag to his mouth, and some of the material was drifting above his couch where the next surge of acceleration would send it flying all over the place. With his feet still held by the webbing Mercer unclipped the sucker from the underside of his couch and went after the stuff, pulling it into the small but powerful vacuum cleaner and leaving in its place a fresh smell of pine trees and heather. Then he helped Stone until he was quite finished, sponged his face and produced a water tube and an anti-nausea pill.

"Sorry about that, Mr. Stone," he said drily, "but there are some people who seem to need double the usual medication."

As he swallowed it, Stone had the grace to blush.

"Mr. Mercer," said Prescott in his earpiece. "Attitude maneuvers are completed. Will you come to control as soon as convenient." His tone was almost polite, which made Mercer feel very uneasy.

His first impulse was to rush to control right away and take what was coming to him for his recent stupid and dangerous display of weightless acrobatics. But ten more minutes' work would complete the rigging of the cabin dividers, and he might just as well go up there with one job done properly, even if he had nearly killed himself doing it. While he was tightening the last rope the screen above him lit up with a clear, sharp, and rock-steady picture of Space Station Three.

A few seconds later he made a slow, careful dive towards the well which connected the passenger compartment with control and rose past the level of the officers' cabin and the enclosed ladder used when the ship was under power or on the ground. He did not bump against anything on the way up, so apparently his weightless movements were becoming more accurate as a result of the last few hours' acrobatics. Even so, he was feeling far from confident as he checked his dive at the entry to control, made sure that his zips were properly fastened and his cap was still on straight, and entered.

Prescott pointed at the empty couch and said angrily, "Lie there, Mercer. Watch the screens or look out of the window. Don't touch anything."

Communications Officer MacArdle and the engineer, Neilson, looked angry as well. So did the Captain. But Collingwood tried to smile as he said, "You did very well, Mercer. But as an entertainer you should avoid over-exposure, and you were in danger of—"

"Fracturing your skull," snapped Prescott.

"I'm sorry about that," said Mercer. "I missed hearing the thrust warning and got caught—"

"You missed hearing it," said Prescott furiously, "because MacArdle was so interested in your performance that he forgot to send it. But even a medical officer with a fractured skull would probably not be enough to put a Hold on this trip. I have never in my life seen a lousier, more slapdash launch—"

"Leave it, Bob," said the Captain tiredly. To Mercer he added, "Mr. Prescott, you may already have noticed, is an astronaut of the old school whose experience goes back to the time before spacetravel was officially declared safe. He is inclined to fuss sometimes."

"At least let Neilson and I eye-ball the drive grids as we're dumping the boosters . . ." began Prescott.

Collingwood's hand twitched as if he had been about

to point at the displays around them, and he said, "Bob, there's no need." He paused, looked at Neilson for a moment, then added, "But to keep you happy, we'll have the station send up close-ups of the withdrawal sequence."

"The definition," said Prescott, "will be too poor to resolve the fine details or show . . . Oh, forget it." He stared angrily at, or maybe through, Mercer, who tried to pretend that he wasn't there.

As he looked at his twin displays—one showing his charges in the passenger module and the other the same picture as they were seeing on their screen—he wondered why Prescott had sent for him if not to give him a ticking off. Mercer's instructor had told him that some medics were never allowed into the controlroom until several weeks of a voyage had elasped. This could have been a compliment, a pat on the back for being a good, hard-working boy—except for the fact that Prescott so obviously did not like him.

Maybe that was why he was here. Prescott did not like anybody, it seemed, and this was his way of showing it. He had told off MacArdle in such a way that the communications officer would be just as angry with Mercer as he was with Prescott. Everybody, even the cool and normally easy-going Captain, was angry with Prescott, and they were only four hours out. Mercer was beginning to wonder if he should have stayed at home.

But then his eyes went to the direct vision port and his doubts faded. The television pictures of this had only been a shadow of the reality and, one way or another, a man could willingly pay an awful lot to see scenery like this.

Chapter IV

Station Three had begun to kill its rotational velocity long before *Eurydice* had been launched. Now it hung motionless like a gigantic, uncompleted wheel comprising six tubular spokes arranged in two diametrically opposed groups of three, and two short tubular sections of rim which linked each group of spokes at the periphery. Unlike its smaller predecessors, One and Two, which were structurally complete and no longer capable of further growth, Station Three was still only a pup.

It would take many years of time and effort, and *Eurydice* and her sister ships would have to pay it a large number of passing visits to donate their boosters, before its thirty spokes and far-flung rim would be completed, because it was the boosters wrapped around the ships' stern and waist sections, emptied of their fuel, which formed the building blocks of the vast wheel. Upwards of four thousand people would inhabit the station then, conducting the more exotic types of research which would ultimately put space and time and gravity to effective use and make slow-burners like *Eurydice* as obsolete as dugout canoes. One of its first, and perhaps easiest jobs, would be to impose a strict control on the Earth's weather.

Later it might give men the stars, or, if not a faster-than-light drive, then the longevity to reach them. It would support and extend the work already being done on the bases of the Jovian moons.

27

That was the kind of work that Mercer wanted to do, among people who freely admitted to being insane for living how and where they did, and who tried to put at least as much into their highly technical culture as they got out of it—a culture which was neither as permissive as Earth's of the past decades or as viciously forbidding as the neo-puritan one which was beginning to replace it.

Mercer was too cynical to believe that the people of the Jovian colonies had built a utopia for themselves; it was simply that they had been very thoroughly screened. There was no mesh in the screen, of course, but it was up to six hundred million miles thick, and anyone who made it through that screen even once had to be someone very special in one way or another—of that Mercer had been very sure, until the crew of *Eurydice* had started leaving clay footprints all over his nice bright illusions.

"Withdrawal sequence starting . . . . . now," said the Captain, arousing Mercer from his day-dream. "Neilson, stand by. MacArdle, ask Three for a long lingering close-up of our tail and be careful how you phrase it." He smiled, looked at Prescott, and stopped smiling as he added, "As soon as we clear the boosters we will roll the ship. All of you take a long, hard look."

Prescott made no comment. He was staring at Neilson, who did not look at all happy.

Mercer divided his attention between the port and his screens as the crew began playing an esoteric game involving the calling out of numbers and groups of initial letters while their fingers tapped illuminated buttons, their quiet voices and off-hand manner not quite concealing their deep concentration on what they were doing. The station TV showed *Eurydice* begin its inching withdrawal from the boosters. As the ship withdrew, it began slowly to rotate.

On the passengers' screen the station was already slipping off the edge, so that they would have nothing to look at until it came on-screen an unguessable number of minutes later. He had no idea how long the visual inspection would take, and the crew were too busy for him to ask, so he switched the passenger screen to the station signal so that they would have something interesting to look at. Then he froze, looking guiltily at Prescott as he wondered whether he was supposed to do things like that without first asking permission.

But Prescott merely nodded and continued with what he had been doing and saying.

Almost imperceptibly, *Eurydice* withdrew from her boosters, like a bolt being slowly unscrewed from an enormous truncated nut. First the bulge of the passenger section twisted out, then the long cylinder directly behind it which housed the free-fall lounge and the water tank containing the reaction mass for the nuclear engine, and finally the long, tapered cowling of the reactor itself. As it drew clear, panels opened and retractable sensors and focusing coils unfolded themselves, breaking up the clean outline.

The wall speaker cleared its throat, and the voice from Three said, "I've got a telescope on you—it gives much better definition than the TV camera. But what exactly am I looking for, fellows?"

The Captain looked at the First Officer without making any attempt to reply.

"Prescott. Nothing in particular, friend. It's just that I'm the worrying type."

Mercer expected a sarcastic retort, but instead there was a long silence, broken when the voice said, "You look good from here, Bob. I'll slip a filter onto this thing and watch while you light your torch. But if you're going to do something melodramatic with your reactor, don't do it too close to the station, huh?"

"Wouldn't dream of it," said Prescott.

On the station picture *Eurydice* drifted away from the boosters, spurting bright balloons of fog as she lined up for the Jovian orbit insertion. Around him, the crew were completing the attitude checks and the Captain was telling the passengers to expect thrust in ten minutes. Mercer concentrated on his own small, overly simple control panel, angling the remote-controlled TV camera on the outer hull to give what he hoped would be a picture of the space-station falling away when they began their burn. The close-up of the tail being transmitted by Three at that time might be a little disconcerting to the uninitiated.

Like himself, he thought drily.

A few seconds before Neilson pulled out his dampers, Mercer switched pictures; then the couch was pushing him gently in the back, and Station Three began to shrink away from the edges of the screen. The enormous structure diminished steadily until it became a tiny, dazzlingly white insect enclosed by the sunset terminator.

"Very artistic," said Prescott. "You'll spoil them if you aren't careful, Mercer."

"A large part of my job," said Mercer stiffly, "is keeping the passengers happy, and I was told that—"

"And a small part of *my* job," Prescott broke in, "is seeing that you do yours correctly. Now, what will be the next item offered for their delight? More acrobatics?"

Mercer shook his head. "Rigging the cabin walls at this stage would interfere with passenger visibility during the survival film, and that should wait until after they've eaten and they begin to realize that they are really in space. So first I introduce them to weightless eating and see that they don't make too big a mess doing it."

"No," said Prescott sharply. "First you switch off the hull TV camera. Station Three will shortly be out of sight, and a continuous picture of a receding Earth might make someone homesick. Then you will announce lunch and then let them get on with it. Ship's officers are supposed to remain aloof from the passengers, Mercer, and running after them too much gives the impression that you are little more than a steward. You are, but *they* must not be allowed to know that. When we cut thrust in two hours from now —for a few minutes only, to test the damper controls— the mess they will have made will be so obvious that with luck they will feel too ashamed of themselves to risk the same kind of mess again. Only then will you go down there—for the first and only time—and clean up. But it would be much better for your image if you chivied one or more passengers into doing it."

"That was how the last medic got himself fixed for the rest of the trip," said MacArdle, laughing, "but then one housemaid wasn't enough for him and he began—"

"Mercer," said Prescott, "what are you waiting for?"

Seething behind what he hoped was a poker face, Mercer killed the picture of the beautiful crescent Earth and spoke to the passengers as he had been directed. He had known people like Prescott for most of his life —teachers and professors and surgeons who had stomach ulcers or bad domestic trouble or who had simply inherited a nasty disposition. There were only two ways to react to people like that: Either ignore them and their continual jabbing until they themselves got tired of doing it, or display a controlled reaction designed to show them that they were not dealing with a sponge that soaked up everything without protest.

"Four hours should be enough to let them eat and get to know each other," Prescott continued, "and not enough to allow arguments to start. You will spend those four hours in your cabin, resting, after which you will see to the tidying up and contrive to introduce the subject of safety and survival in space. You will try to do this without scaring half the passengers to death."

"Just because I've spent most of my life studying for examinations," said Mercer quietly, "doesn't mean I'm stupid."

"There is a difference," said Prescott, just as quietly, "between education and intelligence."

"But I'm not tired," said Mercer, knowing that he

was losing on this exchange but not wanting to admit it.

Prescott sighed. "If you don't go to your cabin," he said, "we won't be able to talk about you behind your back."

As he climbed down to his cabin, very carefully despite the half-G thrust, Mercer was not really surprised to hear Prescott talking to Neilson, with occasional interjections from the Captain, or that the subject of the conversation was far removed from the ship's medical officer. He opened and closed the seals into his cabin, cutting off the sound of voices and feeling like a child dismissed from a room where the conversation was too adult.

Unlike the other officers' cabins, which were fitted with more sophisticated equipment occupying much less space, Mercer's did not give much room for him to move. From the entry lock, the floor grill stretched ten feet to the curved plastic canopy that ran from below his feet to what was nominally the ceiling and gave, in the ship's present mode, a one hundred and eighty degree view of the inside of the outer hull, complete with structural members and brightly colored cable runs. The floor grill, which was just under three feet wide, separated two vertical tiers of bunks, eight on one side and five on the other. This was because the lowest one of the five was Mercer's, and he, being the doctor, needed much more than the twelve inches which divided the patients' bunks.

A passenger unfortunate enough to come down with an infectious disease could be isolated from the living quarters and other patients, because the bunks were each fitted with an individual air supply and a hinged flap which sealed in the patient. Mercer did not suffer from claustrophobia, but he thought that any patient needing to spend more than a few days in one of those bunks would have to be kept under heavy sedation if he wasn't to blow his organic computer.

His own bunk did not have all that much elbow

room, of course, surrounded and overhung as it was by communication and control panels and cupboards containing medication. There was much more than he could ever expect to use, even if a dozen epidemics swept the ship. But to take his mind off Prescott he did a quick check of the medical supplies, then strapped himself into his couch.

But not, he was sure, to sleep. . . .

The buzzer had a low, insistent note that gradually increased in pitch until he signaled that he was fully awake by switching it off. It was replaced by the sound of the Captain's voice, which could not be switched off, ever.

"Mercer, you have been sleeping peacefully, if rather noisily, for the past five and a half hours. During that time your passengers had their first meal and did quite a lot of socializing, so there was no need to wake you. But now the natives are growing restive. As soon as you've eaten go back and see that the place is tidy, then set up for the survival lecture and film. We shall go into cruising mode in just under four hours, so you have plenty of time."

"Yes, sir," said Mercer.

"We are required by law," the Captain went on, "to conduct three survival drills as soon as possible after takeoff, even though nothing has ever gone wrong or, considering the current fail-safe structural philosophies and the multiplicity of back-up systems, is ever likely to. But you know all this. You also know that, to keep the passengers from feeling nervous, the first drill is treated as something of a joke—an amusing film followed by a light-hearted question and answer session.

"Don't frighten them, Mercer. But don't be too much of a comedian, either."

For a few seconds the Captain had sounded exactly like Prescott, Mercer thought. Perhaps he was beginning to understand the reason why the medic before him had tried to make so many friends among the passengers. Or was it his predecessor's behavior with the passengers which was the reason for Prescott and the others treating him as they were doing? It was very hard to know if it was the right or the wrong end of the stick which was being used to beat him.

He was still wondering about it when he returned to the passenger module. The deck was not nearly as untidy as he had expected, nor had the litter been widely scattered by the brief cessation of thrust. Mercer nodded politely to anyone who waved, smiled, or otherwise noticed him as he headed for his couch. He had already decided on the people who would volunteer for the clean-up squad.

"Your attention, ladies and gentlemen," he said, using the module's PA. "By now you should have finished your first meal in space—no doubt with a few accidental spillages here and there—and begun getting to know each other. You will have plenty of time—four months, in fact—to finish getting to know each other, but cleaning up the litter is much more urgent. That is why I would like three of you to—"

It was suddenly like a classroom full of eager pupils with the answer to teacher's question. Mercer shook his head and went on, "I knew that you would all like to help, but to avoid offending anyone I shall pick the three people closest to me, if they have no objections."

They hadn't. Mrs. Mathewson smiled and nodded. Stone nodded without smiling, and Bobby Mathewson was trying desperately to salute, with his arm tangled in webbing, his eyes almost as wide open as his mouth with excitement. Mercer concentrated on the boy.

"We do not salute on this ship," he said gravely, "nor do you call anyone 'sir' except the Captain. Saluting spacemen appears only on television, so you are Mathewson and I am Mercer. Got it?"

Treat a boy like a young man, his instructor had told him, and you won't go far wrong.

Explaining the operation of the cleaners over and over again until he understood it completely was something Mercer could do to the boy but not the two adults. Repeating instructions to them might make them think that he considered them stupid. But this way they would all be sure to get it right without him running the risk of their taking offence. Finally he turned the three of them loose, watched them at work for a few minutes, then returned to his couch to call Mac-Ardle to have the survival film ready to run.

Prescott and Neilson climbed into sight a few minutes later and stood looking around the passenger deck. Mercer went across to them in case they had instructions for him.

Prescott stared at him without speaking. Neilson did not look at him, but said, "I don't understand you. Look at that blonde on couch Eighteen and the Asian on Twenty-three, and you gave away the job to a man, a widow and . . . and her ten-year-old boy. You're missing chances, Mercer."

He spoke softly so as not to be overheard by nearby passengers and without moving his lips, just like a convict in an old-time prison film. Mercer tried to copy the expression and intonation as he replied, "Maybe I *prefer* ten-year-old boys."

Prescott laughed. It was a harsh, unrelaxed sound, probably because it was produced by a mechanism stiff from disuse. Then they left Mercer and continued their climb towards control.

Chapter V

It was a beautifully made film, technically excellent and with a nice balance of animation and actual footage—but it lacked accuracy. Not that it made any deliberate misstatements; it was just that watching the antics of a cartoon character did not give a true picture of a real person's physical and mental capabilities.

A smiling young pseudo-spaceman who had cut his gleaming teeth on a great many TV commercials began by introducing everyone to their ship, talking brightly over performance and payload charts, design philosophy, and an animated staging sequence. Then he began taking the ship apart, literally, into neat, color-coded sections, magnifying each section and detailing its function—control, officers' quarters, passenger lounge and cabins, weightless lounge, reaction mass tank, and the eye-twisting detail of the reactor itself. Mercer's sickbay/cabin looked ridiculously large for one man and thirteen patients, while the quarters of the passengers were unbelievably spacious.

Mercer did not believe, and neither, after a few days, would the passengers.

". . . And now," continued the smiling spaceman, hesitating as if to apologize for wasting their time on non-essentials, "we come to the subject of survival should an emergency arise. No such emergency has arisen in the past, nor, considering the rigorous checks and inspections carried out before every flight, is one ever likely to occur in the future. Nevertheless, we are obliged by the regulations to explain our survival equipment and to give you the chance to practice with it. . . ."

Mercer had already seen the film many times and had listened to much more detailed lectures on the subject. His train of thought branched off onto a different, but nearly parallel, track.

In his line of work human life had always been considered of paramount importance—in theory, at least, a life was valued beyond price. But the cost of protecting the lives of officers and passengers in a spaceship, where every kilo hauled out of Earth's gravity represented enough coin of the realm—anybody's realm—to make every person on the ship comfortably rich from the cradle to the urn, was astronomical. Naturally the price of the passengers' tickets did not defray even a small fraction of the transport bill, much less the extra-weight penalties represented by back-up systems and survival equipment. Those items were conveniently lost in the even more complex systems of government bookkeeping under headings like national prestige, technological spin-off, and assisting the maximum utilization of technically trained manpower.

Human life seemed to grow more and more valuable the farther it was removed from Earth. In space its value was incalculable; in the five-hundred-and-one-thousand-seater transports flying between five and ten miles above the surface it was high; but on surface transport systems the powers that were did not seem to worry too much about lives, passing a few laws about car safety belts, speed regulations and ship radar. As a result, no fare-paying passenger had ever been lost in space, a few hundred a year on average were cremated in metal birds which prematurely stopped flying, and on the surface they mowed each other down with cars in thousands every day.

Mercer had spent two years with an organization which processed road accidents. That was how it referred to itself and the cases it admitted, because far too few of them survived for it to call itself a hospital which cured people. He had grown up in—and was now, he realized, trying to flee—a technologically advanced, ultra-fast and strangely bored society, whose casualties had had the depersonalized, sexless sameness of so many mashed flies. The drunken or drug-ridden or simply bored drivers and the careless or absent-minded or innocent bystanders, when they were separated from the machinery or the machinery was removed from them, could rarely be made presentable by even the most conscientious of morticians.

Mercer's thoughts were taking a very morbid turn. He had long ago discovered that there were no simple answers to complex problems, and the best thing he could do right now was to give all his attention to the survival film while trying not to look openly scornful of the simple answers it was giving to what would be, if it ever occurred, an extremely complex and lethal problem.

The spaceman with the teeth, the cap worn on the back of his head and practically all of his uniform zips undone, was saying ". . . In the unlikely event of such an emergency, the passengers and crew will probably have several hours, or even days, to abandon ship—a process which can, if necessary, be carried out safely and without undue fuss in a few minutes.

"The next stage," he went on, "deals with the mechanics of the abandon ship sequence, showing the basic actions first and then repeating them with certain variations. . . ."

On the screen, the distressed ship developed a faint red halo around its reactor. The halo began to brighten and pulsate, but not quickly enough to really frighten anyone. Further forward, the passenger section continued to spin slowly as it furnished artificial gravity, while the rest of the ship held steady. Then gradually it slowed as braking devices went into operation, making the ship a rigid unit again in the pre-cruising mode. The spinning passenger section had imparted its rotational inertia to the ship as a whole, causing it to spin at half of its original speed.

Suddenly the ship emitted long white cylinders which flung themselves away from the spinning vessel, expanding into large globes as they went. Shortly afterwards, four larger, wedge-shaped sections of the forward structure—the modules containing each officer's cabin—broke away and followed the expanding circle of passenger globes. The remains of the ship, looking warped and lifeless, although not frighteningly so, shrank as the wedges and globes radiated from the wreck and the screen took in a steadily expanding area of space. Finally the ship disappeared. The survival pods applied thrust for a few seconds and began their slow return to the recovery area, until they were grouped like spherical sheep around the officers' segments, which had also returned and were waiting for them.

On the second time around, the sequence went into greater detail regarding the method of entry into the survival pod, its airlock, radio, two-shot thrust motor, and other rather sparse appointments. The final treatment of the sequence, which was too delightfully droll to cause anxiety to anyone, dealt with methods of attitude control in a vehicle which was fitted with only one short-duration and fixed-direction thruster. . . .

". . . Most of you are probably thinking by now that our survivors are being given an awful lot to do," said the space-officer star as his face replaced the image of the survival pods, "or that the globes should contain more sophisticated equipment such as proper attitude control, navigation computers and the like. But you must remember that your survival globe is little more than a life-belt, and that a life-belt cannot be overloaded or it will sink. Believe me, the equipment is adequate.

"It is adequate," he continued in a proud, solemn voice while he tapped his temple very slowly with his right index finger, "because they will each be carrying at least one computer of a type that has been tried and perfected over a million years."

In control, MacArdle brought up the lights and expertly faded out the background music. Mercer stood up, swaying slightly in the low gravity, and looked over his charges. Before he could speak, the passenger called Stone·tapped the side of his head and said solemnly, "He makes me feel proud, and kinda sick."

Me too, thought Mercer. Aloud he said, "Any questions?"

"What I would like to know," said a passenger with Miss Moore stamped on her identity patch, "is why we don't have officers like that on this ship? Why don't *you* relax a little, sir? Can't you smile the way he did?"

"He probably can't," said Mrs. Mathewson, laughing, "because his teeth are real and a bit uneven."

"His eyes look a bit uneven, too," Miss Moore said, "but they are a nice shade of—"

"A trick of the light, m'am," said Mercer hastily, "caused by one slightly thicker eyebrow. But I was inviting questions on survival in space."

"And I was asking one," she replied, looking him straight in the eye. "I was wondering if you had any suggestions on how I can survive the boredom of living for four months in a hermetically sealed can of space-going sardines. I suppose some of the sardines will cooperate in relieving the boredom?"

Mercer nodded and said seriously, "Provision has been made for various forms of individual and group competitions and entertainment. Nothing too strenuous, of course, although it is advisable to take a certain amount of exercise every day to avoid balance and blood pressure problems after we land.

"We have music tapes and films, most of which are fairly recent," Mercer continued. "By that I mean that they have not yet been released for television. There will also be instruction in weightless swimming and ballet, which brings me back to the survival drills. Even though their usefulness is arguable, the three sessions which we are obliged by regulations to stage can be very interesting and often amusing."

The silence began to drag until Stone said, "What we really want to know is what our beautifully-designed individual flight plans say between the lines. There isn't much space between the lines, of course, but if all the rumors we've heard are true, it is very well filled. How about filling in a few of them for us?"

Practically all of the passengers were watching Mercer and listening, or not watching him and listening even harder. He nodded gravely and said, "There is very little to add which is not already there. The rules are few and not at all strict, so that you should be bound only by the dictates of common sense and consideration for each other. You will be living in a restricted space, sharing toilet and amusement facilities, and using cabins which give visual privacy only. It is a good idea to put a little effort into liking instead of disliking the people around you. . . ."

"Love your neighbor?" asked someone.

". . . Apart from this largely self-imposed discipline," Mercer went on, "there are no rules so far as the passengers are concerned, and you will be left pretty much to your own devices. But if some form of individual or group activity proves harmful to the ship or other passengers, the person responsible will be warned and if necessary restrained in sick bay—"

"A fate worse than death, I hope," said Miss Moore.

Mercer nodded. "If you call spending four months in a bunk the size and shape of a coffin under partial sedation a fate worse than death, I'm inclined to agree with you," he said, allowing his irritation with Miss Moore to show for a moment. Mercer knew that he was not supposed to talk as bluntly as this to passengers on the first day out, and that Prescott would probably skin him alive for it. He forced himself to relax and went on, "But that kind of trouble is unlikely to arise among a healthy, civilized group of people like yourselves.

This isn't flattery. You all know how thorough were the medical and psych checks which you had to take before being allowed to book passage."

The trouble was, Mercer thought, that in this degenerate age the mental norms had been stretched to fit some strange psych profiles. About all he really could be sure of was that none of them were or had recently been on hard drugs.

He continued, "With the exception of myself, the ship's officers have their own specialist duties to perform and will intervene only if somebody starts a riot or tries to kick a hole in the hull. A part of my job is to see that you all adapt to shipboard life as quickly and easily as possible, to keep a check on your health, and to instruct you in the use of such items as the swimming facilities and, of course, the survival equipment. I shall not intrude on your social activities even if invited to do so, and you are all free to do pretty much as you please. Have you any questions?

"About the survival film," he added.

Inevitably the Moore woman had a question, the same question with a slightly different slant.

"How will the officers be able to survive the trip," she said, "with nothing to amuse them but computers and textbooks? I realize that you are all highly trained and disciplined supermen, but four months of self-imposed celibacy in a space-going monastery cell . . . I mean, is it necessary?"

Mercer was silent, thinking that the simple answer was that it was not necessary, and that his predecessor's behavior was becoming much more understandable to him. In *Eurydice* temptation was anything but subtle, if this was the kind of question that could come up during the first day's flight. He wondered what Miss Moore did in real life, and he was still wondering and trying to think of a diplomatic reply when Mrs. Mathewson rescued him.

"Maybe our supermen are interested only in superwomen," she said.

Chapter VI

The transition from powered to free flight occurred half an hour later. The anti-nausea medication that he had administered just before takeoff was still doing its job, so that the upsets were psychological and intrapersonal rather than digestive. They came about as a direct result of the transfer of passenger couches from the deck to what had been the walls of the compartment.

Mercer had demonstrated the safe, easy way of performing the operations—by lying face down, held in position by the waist straps only, and allowing the arms and legs to project over the edges of the couch to propel it along, check its progress, or fend off other couch riders on collision courses. But in the weightless condition the couches were too easy to move, and although they did not weigh anything, their inertia was considerable. Set moving in the wrong direction or pushed too hard, they could give a nearby passenger a very painful nudge.

While they were being moved into their new position, Mercer had also to exercise a great deal of discretion regarding who would be occupying adjoining cabins—especially when four or five passengers insisted on adjoining a sixth who did not wish to adjoin with them. Finally, he had to check that the passengers had not positioned their couches across the line of a dividing wall, or over a lighting fixture, or on top of a life-pod escape hatch.

At that stage he signaled control to begin spinning the passenger compartment, and gradually the occupants began to stick with increasing firmness to their new floor. The spin increased until centrifugal force pressed them against the interior of the hull with an apparent gravity one half that of Earth normal. Forward and aft of the passenger sections the compartments that were supposed to remain weightless had begun to rotate in the opposite direction, and Mercer could hear the regular thump of tangential thrusters checking the precession. But none of the passengers seemed worried by the noise—they were too busy laughing and waving at fellow passengers who were apparently standing on the ceiling waving back at them.

Mercer waited for a few minutes to allow them to get used to the sensation, then he made his way to the section of plating occupied by the Mathewsons and asked if he could borrow Bobby. With the boy's help he began distributing the plastic cabin dividers, demonstrating the method of attaching them to the supporting lines so that they formed four taut, plastic walls and a pull-across door-sheet which could be sealed from the inside. By the time he had finished explaining how it was done to the last passenger, the first cabins were complete and he was able to return Bobby to his mother.

"He's been a big help, m'am," he told Mrs. Mathewson, and he was not merely being polite, "but the work has made him a little over-excited, I'm afraid, so I suggest you give him the adult dose of sedative."

He knelt briefly beside her couch, pressed the release stud on a plate that was set flush with the floor, and flipped it back, explaining that the cover was simply for protection during the couch-moving operation and that the recess contained a call-button, microphone and speaker which would enable her to contact him in control or the sick bay if the need should arise.

"But right now I suggest that you take half an hour

getting used to the place and preparing to turn in," he went on. "The cabin walls are opaque but translucent, and we shall be switching off the main lighting in one hour from now. If you want to read, the directional light on your couch will not inconvenience anyone else trying to sleep."

"As for you," he said to the boy, "you can stand down. Don't forget to take your medication. I shall probably need you again tomorrow and I don't want you half asleep on your feet. Good-night, Mathewson."

"Good-night, Mercer," said the boy. His mother smiled and nodded.

In the next cabin he went through the same drill, and in the next. Some of the faces registered, but others did not because he kept thinking about Mrs. Mathewson and the difference a half-G had made to her face, easing the tension lines and rounding out her features and figure. She had looked incredibly young to have a son of ten years. He wondered suddenly if she had escaped from more than just the gravity of Earth. . . .

His last job before leaving for control was to stick name and number patches to the cabin door-sheets and draw up a list of who was where.

It was quiet in the control room, and the expressions on the faces of its occupants made it plain that they wanted it to stay that way. Mercer nodded to Neilson and the Captain—the only two who bothered to look at him—and floated into his couch. He clipped his list to the back of his left forearm and began printing the passengers' names on self-adhesive cards, which he placed beside the numbered lights on his call board. By the time he had finished the vision pick-up showed the passenger compartment in darkness, and his fellow officers were showing signs of breaking their vow of silence.

Beside each numbered call light was a switch which energized the cabin microphones without, of course, acquainting the occupant of the fact. He brought in the Mathewson cabin first, listened briefly to heavy, adult breathing which was too irregular for its owner to be asleep and a childish whisper which was saying ". . . And God bless Mum and Dad and make him the same every day. . . ."

Quickly he flipped off the switch, realizing that Bobby had revealed an awful lot about the Mathewsons in a very few seconds. At least on the ship they would not be troubled by a man who was a different person practically every day of the week.

The other switches brought in the sound of peaceful breathing, and one the silence of an empty cabin. He checked the pickups in the heads, which were also empty, and with visions of a passenger lost in the dark and blundering through fragile cabin walls and waking everyone, he began thumbing the switches, systematically searching for an incipient disturbance.

He did not find it. Instead he brought in a whispered conversation from a supposedly single cabin, which he switched off hurriedly as it was reaching an interesting stage.

"Spoilsport," said MacArdle.

"Sorry," said Mercer. He laughed, ridiculously pleased that someone had at last decided to speak to him.

"There is no necessity for you to remain on duty, Mercer," said the Captain. "Your handling of the passengers has been very good and your own behavior excellent, so far. Why don't you get some extra sleep in your cabin while you have the chance—you have a duplicate board there and the call buzzer is loud enough to wake you should a passenger need attention."

They don't want me around, thought Mercer angrily. Unlike Prescott, the Captain was being polite—even complimentary—in his dismissal, but it was plain that Mercer was not one of the team and that they did not want him hanging around. But all at once Mercer did not want to be sent to bed like a small boy. He was going to be hanging around for the next four months, at least, and the sooner they got used to the idea the better. Besides, the Captain had not actually ordered him below.

He smiled and said, "Thank you, sir. It has been rather hectic down there, but there are times when I find my own company a strain as well. So if you don't mind, sir, I would like to stay for a while and enjoy the atmosphere of sanity and peace."

They did not even look at him, and the silence lengthened, until finally Neilson said drily, "It isn't peace, Mercer—more like a temporary cease-fire."

Prescott stirred on his couch, but it was the Captain who spoke. He sounded polite and friendly and a little absentminded, as if an argumentative medic was only one of his problems.

"It is possible that you will grow exceedingly tired of the control room and the people who inhabit it in the months to come, Mercer," he said. "But you are welcome to stay here, of course, even if there is nothing for you to do. Unless you would like to spend some of the time telling me what you have planned for tomorrow? At one stage, after the cabin construction period, you were apparently organizing card games. Why?"

"Yes, sir," said Mercer. "Two of the passengers seemed to be worried by the survival film, and I changed the subject by telling them that weightless swimming was available to everyone once the ship was in cruising mode. I mentioned cards as being a fair way of deciding who would be the first two people into the pool with me. I'm afraid two at a time is as many as I can handle until I've had a little more experience myself."

"And the survival drill?"

"In the circumstances I thought of delaying them for a few days," said Mercer. "Passenger nervousness can be catching, and my instructor told me that quite a lot of latitude is allowed in the timing of these drills, and that the partial dismantling of cabin walls can be irksome if the passengers are not already a little bored and willing to play a new, if somewhat inconvenient, game.

"Or," Mercer went on, "I could take small groups of less nervous passengers and give them survival instruction until most of them were proficient. That way, the first full-scale drill would not be the shambles that the book says it usually is."

He stopped because the Captain was shaking his head.

"I'm sorry, Mercer," he said firmly, "but I don't agree with that part of the book. I think that I can trust you to carry out the exercise without creating too much alarm among the passengers. The regulations state that survival instruction be given to all passengers as soon as possible after takeoff, and so far as I am concerned, 'as soon as possible' means just that."

Mercer nodded. Obviously Collingwood's conception of the space-going priorities differed from those of the ground-bound, PR-minded type who produced the copy for Mercer's manual.

"Later in the voyage," the Captain went on, "you may stage as many therapeutic survival drills as you think fit, but the passengers must be made aware of the survival procedures at the beginning, not close to the end, of the trip—"

"Eurydice ground control. Do you read?"

The Captain glanced at the speaker grill above his head and said, *"Eurydice. Go ahead."*

"Your signal of 1476 this day querying pulsing and apparent temporary misalignment of your C-Sixes during initial insertion. We have looked at this and can see no cause for concern, especially as your instrumentation gives no indication of malfunction. We don't see that you have a problem, Eurydice."

"We don't have a problem," replied the Captain with just a hint of irritation in his tone, "but we would like an explanation for that few minutes of uneven thrust and we think the answer lies in area C. We will be using the nuclear propulsion system for standby heating only so we are not, repeat, not worried, but—"

"Prescott would like an explanation, I understand."

Reception was too good for there to be any mistaking of the tone, which made it all too plain that ground control knew Prescott of old and considered him to be something of a fusspot. The Captain, Neilson and MacArdle were carefully not looking at the First Officer while they tried to hide their embarrassment. Prescott himself did not appear to be embarrassed or even uncomfortable, and Mercer wondered if he was so sure his point of view was right that it just did not matter what his fellow officers thought of him.

"You already know, of course, that your C-Sixes are sealed units which are very thoroughly tested before assembly. If one of yours is sick, the only way we can check on it is by turning up the maker's worksheets and inspection paperwork. We will get on to that at once and come back to you. Is there anything else not bothering you, gentlemen?"

"Nothing else," said the Captain. *"Eurydice* out."

The silence lengthened, magnifying the tiny sounds made by the life-support and power systems, until Prescott cleared his throat. When he spoke his voice sounded firm and reasonable—perhaps, thought Mercer, this was the nearest that the First Officer could come to apologizing.

He said, "Friend Neilson did not do a complete check of area C for the reasons he has already given—acceptable reasons, to most First Officers. And even if he had carried out the full inspection program, there is still no certainty that the fault—if there is a fault—would have shown up. The chances are that it would not show now even if it is there. But I would still like to have a look—"

"You will stay here, Bob," said the Captain sharply, "while Neilson and I have a look. We'll suit up and go through the passenger section and tank an hour before they are due to waken, so as to avoid worrying them with the sight of two officers in spacesuits. Once I discover the explanation for our initial bumpy ride we shall not discuss it, or even mention it, for the rest of the trip."

This time even Prescott was showing signs of embarrassment, and Mercer was suddenly sorry for him. As a doctor he disliked seeing anyone suffer.

"And Mercer," the Captain went on, "if I tell you too often, or with too much emphasis, not to worry about the things you have just heard, you will probably worry even harder. Let me just say that the problems you will have to face with your passengers will be very much worse than anything that is likely to crop up here. MacArdle, keep an eye and an ear on his panel. You're relieved, Mercer. Good-night."

As he was returning to his cabin, Mercer felt sorry that he had not left sooner. He had thought that they had been trying to exclude him because he was an outsider, a non-member of their very exclusive club, while the truth was that they had an aversion to the presence of a stranger at a family fight.

Chapter VII

Mercer was still half asleep in his couch and squeezing food out of an envelope when he heard the outer hatch open, followed by a polite knock on the inner seal. A few seconds later it opened and Prescott floated in.

"Finish your breakfast and don't get up," he said. "I take it that you will hold the first survival drill as soon as the passengers have eaten and tidied up?"

Mercer nodded.

"Good. But I would like to make a suggestion, or if the polite phraseology gives you the idea that you have some choice in the matter, consider it an order. Demonstrating how to climb into a collapsed life-capsule with three passengers at a time is warm work, so wear your shorts and check on the position of the cabinet containing the bathing gear. You will enjoy a soak afterwards, as well as getting in some practice in weightless swimming before taking on your first two passengers."

"How do I explain wearing swimming shorts at breakfast time?"

"Your problem," said Prescott drily. "Who knows, some of them may enjoy the sight of a splendid, half-naked male animal."

"This male animal runs heavily to skin and bone. . ." began Mercer. But Prescott was already closing the seal behind him.

By the time the passenger breakfast debris had been cleared away his rig had raised a few eyebrows but no comment, and when he reached the stage of rolling up the plastic walls and running the new film, Mercer had forgotten it himself. Prescott ran the film twice—MacArdle being off duty—so that everyone would know how to enter a collapsed life pod, how to do so quickly, and how to help in any late arrivers, or passengers who had not quite got the idea, with the minimum of wasted time and effort. Then Mercer went over the same ground with a slightly different emphasis.

He began briskly: "We are having this drill today, and will probably have another one tomorrow, because we must give at least three survival-instruction sessions as soon as possible after takeoff. That is the only reason. I apologize for the inconvenience it may cause some of you, but it does have its compensations."

He nodded toward the camera pickup, and in control Prescott operated the survival hatch actuators. The covers sprang open, and Mercer went on: "The pods are positioned at equal intervals around the waist of this compartment, and if you simply head for the nearest one there should be no problem. As you saw in the film, the first passenger to enter simply jumps in. The inner seal opens inward and closes automatically when pod pressure begins to build up before release. There is a drop of about eight feet, but under half-G conditions this is no problem. Below your feet there is a plastic bag containing lightweight screens and other bits and pieces used for dividing the inflated pod. Below that is the service module and food store.

"When the first passenger enters the pod," Mercer continued, "he or she will drop until their feet touch the upper surface of the service module. In the uninflated mode the pod walls are folded and the convolutions project inward, so that there will not seem to be enough space for one, much less three people. But these folds are resilient, and the first man in simply presses himself backwards into them, then raises his hands to help the next passenger into the pod."

"The second passenger in does *not* jump," he went

on, "but instead sits on the edge with his legs dangling inside and gripping the hatch coaming with both hands, ready to lower himself inside when the first passenger pulls on his legs. Once inside, the second passenger backs against the first and raises his or her hands to assist the third passenger in the same way so that the three of them fit neatly like a set of three stacked spoons." He cleared his throat. "To begin with, I would like to demonstrate the drill with two volunteers. Mr. Stone and Mrs. Mathewson, would you mind?"

They did not mind, and Mercer jumped in as Number One. Stone followed as Two and got in without any trouble, but he did not press backwards against Mercer firmly enough, so that Mrs. Mathewson found it a very tight squeeze. With much wriggling and elbowing, her feet finally touched the floor of the pod, and a murmur of applause went up from the watchers ringing the opening.

One of them asked seriously, "If there was a real emergency, how much time would we have?"

"You would probably have several hours to get ready," Mercer said, trying to keep the back of Stone's head out of his mouth, "but the drills are always carried out on the assumption that the ship must be cleared within a few minutes, otherwise nobody would ever take them seriously."

He heard a few of them laughing, then another leaned forward to ask, "Does the rule about women and children first still hold in space?"

"No," said Mercer. "The reason for that rule at sea was largely because of the shortage of lifeboats and the skilled manpower needed to launch them. We have more than enough pod space to accommodate all our passengers, and launching is automatic. And now, Mr. Stone, if you will help Mrs. Mathewson out again, we can all get back on deck. I'm beginning to feel like an overdue triplet down here."

That got another laugh, and there were no more

questions about emergencies. He suggested to Stone and Mrs. Mathewson that they go in first with two other passengers each, all of whom would in turn instruct others until everyone had experience of at least one climb into a pod.

"Leave them to fend for themselves," said Prescott suddenly in his earpiece. "I'll keep an eye on them from here while you go aft. Neilson wants you in E-Three, that's the compartment on the other side of the tank. The Captain has a metal splinter in his arm, with complications. Grab your kit and take a look at him."

Mercer licked his lips and said, "Ladies and gentlemen, I'll have to leave you for a few minutes. Just carry on with the practice; you are doing fine."

He did not hurry toward his cabin while he was in sight of the passengers, but made up for lost time when he was not. Within a few minutes he was at the entrance to the tank. From a nearby cabinet he pulled out a mask, visor and air-tank and slipped them on, then stopped.

With an injured arm, the Captain would not want to put on his spacesuit again to come through the tank, so he would need swimming gear, too. And he had said yesterday that he did not want to risk worrying the passengers by letting them see Neilson and himself wearing spacesuits. It might be better to bring along two sets of gear. . . .

"Mercer, hurry it up!" snapped Prescott.

"Just leaving."

The tank lock was big enough to take three people at a pinch, he noted. In the tank itself he fumbled around until he found the light switch and was immediately blinded.

The tank was two-thirds full of the water which the nuclear propulsion system used as reaction mass, and because the ship was in free fall, it had not remained in the lower end of the tank when thrust had ceased. Instead it had spread to fill the whole tank with a glittering froth of bubbles, air pockets and irregular masses of water. It was impossible to see for more than a few yards into the stuff, and it would be very easy to lose orientation. For a few seconds Mercer considered swimming to the wall and pulling himself along the handgrips which projected from it, but that would take time. On the other hand, if he simply kicked hard against the bulkhead behind him and swam, he should reach the other end fairly quickly even if he did not know exactly where he was on the way. The tank was only sixty feet long.

As it happened the trip was far too short, giving him no chance to really appreciate the exquisite sensation of burrowing through clouds of bubbles and of being slapped and buffeted by air pockets and solid clumps of water. He almost forgot the Captain.

"How is it going, Mercer?" said Prescott.

"I'm cycling the aft tank lock now. Everything is fine. The water is nice and warm."

"It shouldn't be."

Mercer had no time to wonder about the warm water because the outer seal had opened and he was looking at his patient.

Both men had their helmets and back packs removed. Neilson was holding the Captain's shoulders, and Collingwood was gripping his right upper arm, where smears of blood were visible above and below his fingers. The complication Prescott had mentioned was that the splinter had entered the Captain's arm while he was outside, and he had suffered a fairly serious decompression—judging by the condition of his eyes and the evidence of bleeding from his nose and ears—before the engineer had pulled him back inside.

Mercer pushed the magnetic studs of his kit against the deck and flipped open the lid.

It rattled at him.

He pulled the radiation counter from its clip and swung around. "You're *hot,* for God's sake! Both of you. Get out of those suits!"

"Mercer, what's happening?"

Before trying to answer Prescott, Mercer took a few minutes to run over the men with his counter—without actually touching them or their suits. The thought of that invisible sleet of radiation going through his unprotected body was enough, without adding the danger of surface contamination. He wanted badly to dive back into the tank and put as much distance between the two poisonously hot officers and himself as the dimensions of the ship would allow.

"Both men have been splattered with radioactive material," said Mercer. He cleared his throat because his voice had sounded an octave too high, then went on, "Neilson is shocked but does not seem to be physically damaged; the Captain's suit was punctured and he suffered a rapid but not explosive decompression. There is bleeding from the ears and nose, some boil-off from the tear ducts, some lung damage, too, judging by his difficulty in breathing—"

"Captain, what happened?"

"He probably can't hear you," said Mercer. "But surely the answer can wait. We have to get them out of the suits fast. The radioactive material must be adhering very loosely to the suit fabric. It could come loose and drift about waiting for us to breathe it in—we may already have breathed it in. Can you come down here? I need help."

"You're right, the answers can wait," Prescott replied calmly. "And sorry, I can't help you nor can MacArdle—our power instrumentation is beginning to look very sick and we'll be busy for a while. Neilson, do a fast undress of the Captain and yourself. It means ruining the suits, but nobody will be able to wear them for about fifty years anyway. Move, and do exactly as the Doctor orders."

Mercer looked at Neilson, who still seemed dazed, and said clearly, "Strip off your spacesuits, coveralls, everything, as quickly as possible. Try not to contaminate the skin while taking them off. Have you got that? Then put on the air-tanks, breathing masks and shorts.

Inside the tank try to create as much turbulence as possible with your hands and feet to wash off any hot stuff that may have stuck to your skin. . . ."

He broke off, wondering why he had thought it necessary to mention the shorts at a time like this. Was he hoping that this sudden emergency might not be as serious as it seemed, that the ship's supermen would cure their vessel's ills while he performed the same service for its Captain, and that in a few days' time the problem would have shrunk to lesser importance than that of allowing two ship's officers to appear before the passengers minus their shorts? Was he, in fact, trying hard to reassure himself? The answer was a very definite "yes."

Neilson was performing a weightless adagio dance with the Captain as he began withdrawing Collingwood from his suit. Mercer went forward to help, but stopped when the engineer said sharply, "Don't touch. I have gauntlets and you haven't. This won't take long —be ready with his breathing gear."

When Neilson pushed the Captain towards him, Mercer put his mouth close to Collingwood's ear and said loudly, "I'm dressing you for the tank, sir. You can spend a few minutes getting used to the breathing mask before we go in. Try not to cough." By the time he had slapped a temporary patch on the arm wound Neilson was crowding into the lock behind them, carrying a large, cylindrical case with a handle on it.

"You take this, Mercer," he said, pulling up his mask to speak. "You'll need it later. I'll take care of the Captain."

But the Captain was trying to take care of himself, even though his eyes were still squeezed shut and blood continued to leak from his nose and ears, kicking out with his feet and moving the water around his body with his good hand. When they went through to the passenger section he was even able to walk. He looked a bit unsteady, but no more so than the passengers, who were experiencing their second day in weight-less conditions. Neilson, without being too obtrusive about it, was guiding the Captain while pretending to fuss with his airtank. Mercer had plugged the Captain's ears and nose with cotton when they came out of the tank and had left the visor in place instead of pushing it onto his forehead, and the condensation on the inside of the glass hid his eyes from the passengers.

"Both of you go to my cabin," he told Neilson quietly. "Put the Captain in bunk Three, it's shielded, and stay there yourself. Don't risk contaminating the control room until I've checked you again. I'll be with you in a few minutes."

He stopped then and looked at the passengers around and above him. Their clothing was disheveled, their hair mussed, their faces red, and most of them were smiling. With an effort, Mercer made his face do the same, but before he could speak there was an interruption.

"I would like a swim," said Miss Moore loudly. She looked much more mussed than any of the others, but seemed quite happy about it as she went on, "You *promised* us a swim today, and you three have been in—"

"Yes, m'am," said Mercer quickly. "These two officers are the Captain and the Engineer. Rank has its privileges, and the survival drills must come first. But right now I suggest that you replace the—"

"Negative, Mercer, negative," said Prescott sharply. "For the time being I want the pod hatches open and the cabin dividers out of the way. Do you understand?"

Some sort of accident aft, warm water in the tank when it should not have been warm, the engineering instrumentation looking sick, and the passenger compartment to remain ready for evacuation. Mercer understood.

He held his smile in place and went on, "I mean, of

course, *resume* the drill. You all know what to do now. Just try to do it a little faster. Try hard."

"If we tried it two at a time," said one of the men, "it might be easier to get the hang of it."

"Three to a pod," said Mercer firmly. "The third passenger is a necessary requirement, to act as chaperone."

They were still laughing as he hurried after the Captain and Neilson. Mercer wanted to tell them to stop laughing, and to tell them the reason why they should stop laughing and instead start learning to survive as fast as they could. But the rules did not allow that. Terminal cases were never told they were going to die until, or unless, all hope was gone.

Chapter VIII

In the sick bay, Neilson insisted that Mercer dress properly before he touched either of his patients; he quickly opened the container which the doctor was still carrying and began helping him into the anti-radiation garb which it held—loose pants that came up to his armpits, a combination hood and cape, elbow-length gauntlets, and heavy periscopic goggles. The material was flexible but heavily leaded. In free fall conditions the weight did not matter, but the inertia made it difficult to initiate a rapid movement and just as hard to stop it.

Neilson told him that the rig was used while checking hot sections of the reactor in areas that were pressurized. Mercer thought that he had felt cooler in quite a few turkish baths, but the feeling of protection which the rig gave him more than outweighed that disadvantage.

The Captain was the more serious case of the two, and Mercer felt guilty about treating the engineer first. But with luck Neilson would need only simple medication—something to steady him without making him sleepy—to be fit for duty, while Mercer did not at the moment know what, if anything, he could do for the Captain. So he went over Neilson with his radiation counter, square inch by square inch, so intently that when Prescott's voice sounded in his earpiece he nearly lost the counter.

"Can I have the Captain and Neilson back, Mercer?"

"Neilson is clean and fit for duty," Mercer replied, "but the Captain is a more complicated case—Neilson will tell you about him when he sees you—and will need a longer examination." He hesitated for a moment, wanting an answer but not trusting himself to ask the question in case his fear would show, then went on, "How much time am I likely to have?"

Prescott also hesitated, and Mercer could imagine him trying to decide whether to be reassuirng or truthful. Finally he spoke:

"The way it looks now, Mercer, nothing sudden or dramatic is likely to happen for at least another hour, perhaps two. If the situation changes, you will be the first to know."

Mercer thought that the First Officer had sounded both truthful and reassuring, which in the present circumstances was quite a trick. He turned, stuck his medical kit at a convenient height, and strapped his feet securely to the floor grill beside the Captain's bunk.

He had to begin by treating the symptoms rather than the multiple ailments in order to make the Captain as comfortable as possible before the curative treatment could begin—always supposing that a cure was possible with non-specialized instruments and medication while operating in weightless conditions for the first time. Speaking loudly but reassuringly, he managed to get Collingwood to relax his eyelids and then open his eyes. Mercer did not like what he saw, and the Captain, of course, could see nothing.

"Your eyes are swollen as a result of the decompression, sir," Mercer said clearly, putting his face as close to the Captain's ear as the leaded hood and goggles would allow. "You can't see at the moment and will not be able to do so until the incidental damage in the area has had a chance to repair itself.

"I'm going to apply some cream which will make your eyes more comfortable and aid the healing," Mercer went on, "then I want you to shut them and keep them shut for a few days to give it a chance to work. I shall probably have to repeat the application until you have specialist attention. But now I'm going to pad and lightly bandage your eyes, mostly to remind you not to use them."

He attended to the damaged ear-drums next, saying that no doubt MacArdle would be able to modify one of the intercom earpieces to serve as a hearing aid for the remainder of the voyage. Then he checked for bladder and anal damage, leaving the lungs—where the major damage was most likely to have occurred—until last.

By then Collingwood was not a prepossessing sight. The minor blood vessels lying just under the skin in areas where his spacesuit had not been a close fit had distended or ruptured due to the decompression. The Captain looked as though a gang of professional thugs had worked him over or he had been the victim of a tattooist gone mad.

"Would you mind coughing into this, sir?" said Mercer, after he had sounded the lungs with his stethoscope. He was beginning to get used to the idea of rotating his weightless patient instead of moving around himself.

"I've been trying not to cough for hours," said the Captain.

"Now you have permission, sir. And spit, too, if you can."

Mercer examined the results, feeling glad that the Captain could not see them. Aloud, he said, "There is some evidence of lung damage—not unexpected, but it could have been very much worse. You must have expelled most of the air from your lungs as soon as you realized that your suit had been pierced."

"Yes, Doctor—screaming bloody murder. It hurt me. It still hurts me."

"I'm sorry about that, sir," Mercer replied, "but I had to be sure that your heart and lungs were in shape to take a general anesthetic if one was necessary. As things are, a local will do fine. In a few minutes you won't even know that you have an arm, much less one with a hole in it."

While the injection was taking hold, Mercer strapped the Captain firmly into his bunk, tying down his legs, arms and waist, but so as not to constrict his chest. With the radiation counter keeping a raucous accompaniment, he began to probe the wound.

An hour later he was still probing, and two tiny specks of radioactive metal were wasting their energies on the walls of a lead container, when the cabin speaker came to life with a voice that Mercer did not recognize at first. But then he realized that it was the strange sound of Prescott being polite.

"Ladies and gentlemen, the survival-drill period is now at an end. If you will kindly stand clear of the pod hatches I shall close them and allow you to replace your cabin dividers and have lunch. Thank you."

Prescott did not have a personal message for Mercer —obviously he was supposed to read between the lines of the P.A. announcement, which made it clear that the ship was not nearly as sick as had been thought at first.

He treated and dressed the arm wound, which was now clear of contaminated metal. But the radiation counter still did not sound happy, and he soon found out why.

There were two other points of emission, separated by a little more than three inches, deep in the right lung. Probably he had inhaled them while Neilson was pulling him out of his spacesuit; or one of the pieces could have been carried from the site of the arm wound through the subclavian vein and superior vena cava, heart, and pulmonary artery, doing a fair amount of damage every inch of the journey. Now they lay like two tiny incendiary bombs, slowly burning the life out of the surrounding tissue and killing off red corpuscles by the hundreds.

With the medical facilities available in the ship, Mercer could not remove them—more accurately, with his relatively crude radiation counter he could not pinpoint their position close enough to dig for them without killing the patient. And if he did not remove them, they would kill him anyway in a matter of time. Mercer did not know whether the available time would stretch beyond the scheduled end of the trip or if he would have to request Prescott to abort and head for home.

If this sort of situation arose at sea, it was a simple matter to return to port or whistle up a chopper with a medical crew on board and transfer the casualty to a shore hospital. But *Eurydice* was using the orbital speed of Earth and the gravity of the Sun to help speed her on her way, and she might not carry enough reaction mass to kill her present velocity, build up enough speed for a fast return, and then kill that velocity, too.

Only Prescott could give him those answers, and the first thing he would want to know was the time available for the Captain. By keeping the patient under close observation for a few days and checking on the cumulative effects of the radiation, Mercer thought that he could probably make a rough estimate, but he would also have to make allowances for the effect of the decompression damage and any psychological factors that might aid or retard recovery.

Physically, Collingwood was in very good shape, and psychologically, well, Mercer remembered the hostess who had ridden with him in the coach to the launching pad—the smiling, generous, beautiful girl who was the Captain's wife—and decided that there would be no problems with the patient about not wanting to live.

While he was still thinking about the Captain's wife and remembering how she had asked him to look after her husband and everyone else, Mercer administered a sedative shot and, after some hesitation, a three-day PC which would render the patient less excitable, more fatalistic, and willing to accept suffering without complaint. He waited until the Captain was asleep, then closed his bunk and slid it into its recess. After that he took off and stowed away his protective clothing and changed into his uniform, carefully checking the zips and the angle of his cap.

The ship might have been ready to blow up a few hours earlier, but somehow he did not think that this would be an acceptable excuse to Prescott for sloppiness of dress. Before leaving the cabin he switched over the bunk mike so that he would be able to monitor the Captain's breathing from his position in control.

Prescott gave him a few minutes to settle into position, turn up the gain on the Captain's monitor, and check on the passengers through the vision pickup. Most of them were in their cabins, but there was a small group aft watching the antics of two girls who were flapping their arms and pretending to be birds in the weightless section between the passenger compartment and the tank. The mikes brought only the sounds of the two human seagulls and amused noises from the watchers.

"We heard you talking to the Captain," said Prescott finally. "It sounded encouraging. Is he going to be all right?"

"He isn't fit for duty and won't be for the rest of this trip," said Mercer carefully. "As for being all right, that depends very largely on the health of the ship. How is your patient?"

Prescott looked at him sharply, then said, "At present we have two additional options to that of abandoning ship. The first is that we proceed as originally planned. This will necessitate testing the nuclear reactor briefly to make sure that it will work properly during deceleration at the other end. This additional spurt will mean minor course corrections and will eat into our safety reserve of reaction mass, but not significantly. The second option is to abort the trip and head for home as quickly as possible. This will leave us with no reserves at all.

"So you can see that the ship is very sick but should

survive, barring complications," Prescott ended. "How does this affect the health of your patient?"

Mercer briefly described Collingwood's condition, the treatment and medication he had been able to give, and explained the difficulty of giving an accurate prognosis until he had a chance to observe his patient over a longer period. He went on, "I have no idea of the intensity or duration of the radiation that he was exposed to at the time of the explosion which punctured his suit—"

"It wasn't an explosion, Doctor," said Neilson suddenly. "Think of holding a pencil in each hand and pressing the unsharpened ends together, hard. So long as the pressure is directed evenly along the axes of the pencils, nothing happens, but the slightest lateral pressure can result in broken knuckles. When the Captain began removing the control-rod retaining sleeve. . . Well, he said that we were to stay off the suit-to-ship frequency because he did not expect to find trouble, and he was afraid that not finding it would make me say something which might embarrass Prescott. When it happened I didn't even remember the radio until we were inside, and then I did not know how serious it was until you started yelling that we were hot. . . ."

"This isn't an official enquiry, Neilson," Prescott broke in. "I have already tried to tell you that the blame for this mishap lies with the final assembly and inspection people—they fitted six perfect actuator rods, except that one of them was the wrong size. I doubt if even pre-launch inspection would have caught that one —they look for the minor errors, the tiny ones which can sometimes slip past the inspectors farther up the line, not major structural blunders like this. You stood very little chance of spotting it even if you had suspected that something was wrong, and as you well know, my earlier displeasure with you was caused by your not properly inspecting an entirely different system, which has not given any trouble.

"If there is an official enquiry," Prescott went on,

"you will be commended by me for your fast rescue of an EVA decompression case. So stop craving absolution for someone else's sin, concentrate on your board, and shut up. Go ahead, Doctor."

Mercer nodded. He was beginning to realize that Prescott was a fair rule-of-thumb psychologist, even if his thumb was somewhat calloused. Neilson had obviously been feeling guilty about the accident, and now the only person who might still have thought him responsible—Mercer himself—knew otherwise. The final blast was just a reminder, also reassuring in the present circumstances, of who was boss and the bearer of the ultimate responsibility.

"If the trip proceeds normally," Mercer resumed, "he might not survive it if the radiation was intense, or he may survive with a rapidly developing leukemia, which will need frequent transfusions to keep him alive. No doubt there will be donors of the right blood type among the passengers, but while those two fragments of metal remain in his lung—"

"There is no chance at all of digging them out?"

"They are tiny," said Mercer. "It would be like spooning out strawberry jam to find two specific pips."

"Please," said MacArdle, looking slightly sick.

"We don't carry the specialized equipment needed to treat him," Mercer said seriously, "and his condition is grave enough to warrant turning back, if you have the reaction mass to do so."

"We have," said Prescott, "and we will."

Mercer could not hide his relief, even though a fair proportion of it was for his patient. He said, "Not a direct return and landing, sir. Reentry deceleration might kill him, and if he did survive it, recovery would be much slower in a surface hospital. Station Three have all the facilities in their advanced medicine section to put him right."

"Station Three," said Prescott drily, "can cure my patient, too."

Chapter IX

"Eurydice control. Do you read?"

Mercer had his ears on the Captain's respiration and his eyes on the passenger vision pickup, which showed a fair amount of socializing going on in the module and two couples dancing—mixed wrestling might have been a better description—in the weightless section forward of the tank. He did not pay much attention to the exchanges between Prescott and *Eurydice* ground control —they were too technical for him in any case—until the acid tones of the First Officer became noticeably more caustic.

". . . A combination of minor oversights, none of which would have been individually troublesome," Prescott was saying. "Next thing you'll tell me that they could have happened to anybody."

"The man will be fired, of course, with the others who missed his slip-up. But it was basically a clerical error, and he was under stress at the time. A domestic problem was worrying him, his wife was expecting their first—"

"I hope," said Prescott savagely, "that she bore him a litter of lizards. But I'm more concerned with effects right now. Just as soon as possible we shall apply full thrust. But first, before we swap ends to decelerate, I must know if the nuclear propulsion system is safe. The accident knocked out most of our sensory circuits in that area and, although the remaining instrumentation gives a confused but not exactly dangerous picture, I'm worried about that slight rise in temperature reported in the water tank."

"I'm not questioning your decisions, Prescott, but aren't you over-reacting to all this? The chances are that you will have no further trouble and that the damage is easily reparable. Maybe the Captain's condition is not quite so serious as you think, and in the heat of the moment Mercer may have mistaken the temperature of the tank water and—"

"Unlikely," said Prescott. "There have been a few hot moments since and he hasn't—"

"Very well, Prescott, carry out your abort. We'll allow you half an hour to swap ends—no point in wasting time if you are set on doing it—and give you the numbers for full deceleration and insertion into the return orbit. Do you still want the recovery ship team on standby?"

"Don't ask stupid questions."

"Very well. Eurydice control out."

Prescott took a deep breath and turned to Mercer. "You may have thought that I was about to compliment you back there. Don't set too much store by that—I just can't abide outsiders criticizing one of the family, even a new, untrained, foundling member like you.

"But I've a job for you," he went on. "Go back and recheck the tank temperature. You'll find insulated bottles in the bulkhead locker beside the outer seal. Take one. You will see that it has a snap fastening at the neck, that it is double-walled, and that there is a thermometer and a yellow disc, which changes color in certain circumstances, between the walls.

"Go into the lock chamber," he continued. "No need to go into the tank itself at this stage until we have some idea of how much radioactive contamination you left behind after your first bath. Open one of the inner valves, which are plainly labeled with operating instructions, and press the neck of your bottle against the outlet and keep it there until it is nearly full. In free fall the water will not pour out, so you may have to wait a few minutes for it to fill. . . ."

"I should do this," said Neilson suddenly. "After all, I'm still dressed for the job."

"Don't think I haven't noticed," said Prescott sourly. "Pull up your shorts, dammit. I have enough problems on this ship without having my sensibilities blasted by the sight of your hairy navel. And I don't want you or your eyes to leave that board. MacArdle will monitor the Captain's breathing and watch your board, Mercer, so move."

As he would not have to go into the tank itself, Mercer did not bother to change, but he put on a purposeful expression and pretended not to notice the passengers who spoke to him on the way. The weightless dancers were not noticing anyone but each other. He found an insulated bottle and entered the chamber quickly, pressed the mouth against the outlet and began turning the valve.

The metal felt very warm.

Suddenly the bottle thumped against the palm of his hand. He stared at it stupidly, realizing that it was already full and that it should not have filled so quickly. As he withdrew and sealed the bottle, steam and scalding gobbets of water spurted from the outlet, filling the chamber with a hot, blinding fog. Mercer let go of the bottle, wrapped his hand in his cap and twisted shut the outlet valve, while with his other hand he groped for the evacuation button. He heard the combination suction pump and air blower—the only means of rapidly emptying a compartment full of weightless water—making rude, gurgling sounds.

But the chamber did not clear completely—steam and a fine spray of scalding droplets were spurting from the edges of the inner seal. Mercer retrieved his cap and test bottle, whose thermometer showed a temperature close to boiling point and a disc which had turned from yellow to muddy brown. He felt like a half-boiled lobster with an icy cold lump of fear in its belly. Even though he did not know what exactly was happening, he did know that it was deadly serious and that he had to get back to Prescott fast.

The passengers outside had other ideas, however. As soon as he came out they surrounded him, laughing and trying to grab him.

"There's a black crow among the lovebirds," said one of the men. "A wet, black crow."

"That isn't fair," said one of the girls. "You promised us a swim, and now you've had two and—"

"With your *clothes* on!" added the other girl, who had succeeded in grabbing his ankle.

He wanted to yell at her to let go or he would kick her pretty, laughing face, that he had no time for horseplay at a time like this. But instead he said, "No m'am, space-washing. I dump my wet uniform in a lock, open it to space and the moisture boils off. It takes out the wrinkles, too. Excuse me, I mustn't catch cold . . ."

When he entered the control room a few minutes later, Prescott, with one hand gripping the engineer's headrest, was hovering over Neilson's board. He said, "Mercer, you do *not* launder your uniform in that incredible fashion, unless you don't mind ice crystals in your underpants—and your ability to lie convincingly under pressure worries me. . . ."

He broke off as he saw Mercer's face, then put out his free hand for the bottle.

"It's hot," said Mercer.

Prescott's features went stiff. "In both senses of the word." He handed it to Neilson and added, "Well?"

The engineer took one look, then said very calmly, "This damn board is half dead and the rest of it is sick. Getting no response at all from the sensors usually means a complete power cut-off or a simple circuit failure. This tells me that it is circuit failure; probably the cable looms are melted through, and the amount of heat conducted through the stern to the tank tells me that we have a reactor meltdown situation. At the moment the dampers are in just far enough to give power for lighting and life-support, but they aren't locked, and now I can't lock them. When the rod actuators melt they will pop out and the reactor will go critical."

"Have you enough power," said Prescott, "to engage with the passenger module?"

Neilson nodded.

"Then do that."

Prescott swung himself into his couch as the control room began gradually to share the spin and apparent gravity of the passenger section. He unclipped the public address mike, paused for a moment, then said calmly, "Attention, ladies and gentlemen. Please stand clear of the survival pod hatches; they will open in five seconds. This is not a drill. We are preparing to abandon ship."

It sounded too frighteningly final. Too much was happening too quickly, and Mercer desperately wanted to go back in time, if only for a few minutes, to give himself a chance to assimilate it. Inanely, he said, "When I was in the tank chamber the inner seal looked as if it might—"

There was a loud thump, and the edge of the door he was gripping jerked under his hand. On the passenger view-screen he could see steam filling the passage leading to the tank.

"It just has," said Prescott, "but the outer seal is much stronger and should hold for a while. See what you can do for your passengers."

Mercer had trouble negotiating the normally weightless passage to the passenger compartment because the gravity-free forward and stern sections were now sharing the rotation of the central module. This was necessary if the four big, widely-curving supports, which carried the power and control links fore and aft as well as allowing the passenger section to rotate independently of the rest of the ship, were not to snag the life pods on their way out. The effect on Mercer in that narrow passage was that his feet were pulling one-eighth G while his head and chest were weightless, and Coriolus force was giving him an extra twist just for luck. But Prescott was not allowing time for anyone to think, much less feel confused.

"Attention ladies and gentlemen. The survival pod hatches are now open. Please board three to a pod in a brisk but orderly manner, just as you did during the drill. The hatches will be sealed prior to pod ejection in five minutes."

Mercer was in the passenger section by then, furiously running over in his head the emergency instructions which he had memorized only hours earlier. He added loudly, "Don't forget to leave behind all personal effects which are metal or have sharp edges, such as manicure scissors, jewelry with large stones, or anything which might puncture the fabric of the survival pod. Don't worry about losing them—you will be fully compensated for their actual or sentimental value with no quibbling. . . ."

Which was a *stupid* thing to say at a time like this, thought Mercer. It had just popped out without thinking, and he could just imagine what Prescott would have to say about it. Unless, of course, his subconscious had been working even if the rest of his mind had not, and it had decided that appearing to worry over trifles at a time when all hell was breaking loose was also an effective means of giving reassurance.

But suddenly all such subtle methods of reassurance became superfluous as the outer seal of the tank began to give. Steam billowed into the passenger module, cutting visibility to a few yards, while a high-pitched whistle made it just as difficult to hear. Mercer leaned toward the nearest couch mike.

"Control, give me maximum lighting, please."

Someone screamed as the lights went up to full strength, probably thinking that there had been an explosion. As a result, the passengers who had been standing around, too stunned by events to move, began piling into the pods. The process was not orderly but it was fast. He stumbled into three of them who were trying to get into a pod at the same time, dragged two of them back—no effort in quarter-G conditions—and fed them in at five second intervals. A few yards farther on there was a woman rolling up the cabin dividers.

"We won't be using them again, m'am," he shouted. "Get in your pod."

He continued from pod to pod, not wasting time on words when a good hard push would serve instead, but usually finding that the heads and shoulders were disappearing with satisfactory rapidity.

"Anyone who hasn't found a place?" he called. "Speak up, please."

"Bobby! Where's *Bobby. . . ?*"

He glimpsed a moving shape in the fog and went after it. The extra lighting was making the thickening clouds of steam more dazzlingly opaque now and not helping visibility at all. He gripped Mrs. Mathewson by the arm and pulled her toward the nearest hatch opening.

"Have you room for one more?"

"No, full up." replied a voice from inside.

Mercer swore, not believing it. Still gripping Mrs. Mathewson, he knelt down and reached into the pod with his free hand. He felt the tops of four heads. They certainly were full up.

"Mercer, hurry."

He ignored Prescott's voice in the earpiece and that of the distraught girl on the other side as he moved to the next pod and repeated the question. The white blur of a face appeared, then a pair of hands.

"Listen, m'am," he said as gently as he could while shouting. "Bobby is safe. People feel very protective towards children, and he was probably first into someone's pod minutes ago. So just . . . No, leave go of my neck. He'll be all right, I promise you. . . ."

He was holding her by the armpits over the open pod, and a pair of hands were trying to pull her in.

Suddenly he kissed her steam- and tear-streaked face. She was so startled that she lost her grip on his neck and disappeared into the pod.

I've been doing a lot of things without thinking today, he thought, and they all seem to turn out right. But just then he badly wanted to dive into the nearest pod, kick and claw his way to the bottom no matter how many other people were in it, and wait until Prescott flung them clear. The whistle of escaping steam had taken on a deeper, burbling tone, which probably meant that the seal was ready to give and there would be a major steam explosion at any moment. And as he moved from pod to pod, shouting for anyone who had not found a place to call out, he found himself splashing through half an inch of near-boiling water.

The hatch lips were only an inch above deck level. The fog was unpleasantly hot and it was difficult to breathe. He filled his lungs carefully, cupped his hands around his mouth and shouted, "Is everyone aboard the pods?"

From somewhere in the fog a voice called shrilly, then began to cough. Mercer headed for the sound until a short, grey ghost loomed out of the dazzling mist. It said tearfully, "I'm looking for my mother."

Mercer grabbed the boy by the waist and splashed towards the nearest open hatch. There he turned him upside-down and said very clearly, "Your mother is safe, but her pod is overcrowded so you'll have to take this one. Wriggle your way to the bottom as fast as you can—there isn't much time and nobody will object when they know who it is. You'll probably have to take charge of this lifeboat, Mathewson. Good luck and in you go."

"Room for a small one," he called into the pod. There was no reply, but then he had not really been asking a question.

When Bobby's heels disappeared, he turned so that his back was to the sound of the monstrous steam whistle astern. It was the only means of getting his bearings because his eyes were closed and his cap was pushed over his nose and mouth to make it a little easier to breathe. When he stumbled against a couch he remembered something and bent down.

"Prescott, they're all aboard."

"Return to control."

It was slightly cooler in the passage leading to the control room—he did not need his cap to breathe through, and he could even see a short distance, specifically a recessed basket marked Crew Laundry, with a couple of rolled-up coveralls inside. He took one set as he passed.

The whistle from the stern was becoming louder and deeper, but it was not as loud as the clang of the survival pod hatches going down.

Chapter X

"Close the door and take your couch," said Prescott. "We won't be going anywhere for a few minutes."

Nobody seemed to be doing anything except waiting. Mercer did as he was told and watched the steam that had come in with him being shredded and sucked in by the air conditioning. It was so quiet that he could even hear the Captain's breathing. The silence was frightening him, giving him a chance to do nothing but think.

"Neilson," he said suddenly, tossing the soiled coveralls towards the engineer, "it's hot out."

"Bless you," said Neilson. "With my fair, Nordic complexion I boil easy." He looked enquiringly at Prescott.

The First Officer nodded. "Put them on. And shut up, both of you."

"Eurydice Control. We have a suggestion here that you retain your passengers and dump the sick reactor. Venting the tank astern should nudge it away from you, and you will have a fairly comfortable ship to live in until the recovery vessel reaches you."

Prescott looked at Neilson, who turned down the corners of his mouth.

"Eurydice. We have already looked at that idea. Negative. We have virtually no control of any stern system other than the tank emergency vent." Prescott leaned towards his board, paused, then went on, "We

77

are releasing the survival pods . . . now. Time is 1605 plus fifteen seconds, launch zone."

"We copy, Eurydice."

Mercer twisted around to the direct vision port. He could see five deflated pods tumbling away from the ship, looking like stubs of discarded cigarettes. They were falling away at eight feet per second, the velocity imparted by the passenger module's centrifugal force of one-quarter G. But they shared *Eurydice's* forward velocity, so that they kept pace with the ship, merely spreading out like a ring of receding moons.

Suddenly they appeared to swell and come nearer, but it was only an illusion created by their plastic canopies pressurizing to full size. Still receding, they began to slide slowly past the viewport.

The crew survival sections were much closer to the ship's axis than had been the pod housings, so that to release them with the same velocity away from the ship, *Eurydice* had to increase her spin to compensate.

"More trouble," said Neilson quietly.

"Go ahead, Eurydice."

"The tangential jets are spinning us up to release speed, but the circuit for cutting them just died. I can't shut them down. We'll have to release exactly on the pip, twelve minutes and seven seconds from . . . now."

"We copy."

"Set the timers to release automatically at that time," said Prescott. "Do you still have control to the stern emergency vent?"

Neilson showed crossed fingers and said, "At the moment, yes."

"Set a timer on it to vent ten seconds after we release. Can you estimate the strength and duration of the thrust and the acceleration to terminal velocity, allowing for the absence of the crew segments, rendezvous marker, and the reducing weight of water in the tank?"

"Some of the water has already vented into the passenger section," Neilson replied, "so it will stay with the ship and boil off very slowly. But I have no way of telling how much there is."

The conversation was so quiet and matter-of-fact that Mercer wanted to shout and break things. But it was quiet because the control room door was tightly closed and the mikes in the passenger section had been switched off. Apparently, calmness could be just as contagious as panic, because he found himself saying quietly, "Between the time the tank's outer seal gave way and I left the passenger section eight minutes ago, the water had risen half way up the rims of the survival hatches—about half an inch. Does that help?"

"It's better than making a blind guess," said Neilson. "Let's see, we know the deck area of the passenger section, and we have a rough idea of the volume of water covering it, but add a little for the water content of the steam—"

"Eurydice Control. Please clarify. What are your immediate intentions?"

"Eurydice," Prescott replied. "We are not sure if we have a pile meltdown or a bang situation. If a bang, we want to be as far away from it as possible, and we also want the radioactive debris to be well clear of the pickup area when the recovery ship arrives. Since our reactor controls are out, we propose venting the tank through the stern and bypassing the reactor. Structural heating is such that we should have a crude steam jet which will accelerate the ship ahead and, I hope, clear of the survivors before the bang. Neilson?"

"Roughly two feet a second rising to three as she sheds reaction mass," said the engineer. "If the structural heating extends to the passenger module, the water there will also vaporize and vent through the stern as well, but the additional thrust will be negligible."

"We understand, Eurydice. The recovery ship countdown is now at minus ninety-six hours and three minutes. It will be out there in just over five days."

"You *don't* understand," said Prescott sharply. "We

don't need a fast rescue. Take your time and check the nuts and bolts. You cannot risk a launch until *Eurydice* has blown or is a safe distance ahead of us."

And if it went critical before then, Mercer knew, there would be no point in launching the recovery ship at all.

MacArdle said, "Rendezvous beacon launched at sixteen twelve and eight seconds. Minimal lateral velocity—just enough to let it clear the steam jet."

"*Copy.*"

"Timers set and checked," said Neilson.

"Beacon radiating," said MacArdle.

Prescott took a deep breath and looked quickly around the control room. He said, "We shall all feel a little safer in our cabins. Neilson and MacArdle, get going. Mercer, hold a moment."

Steam was coming from the air conditioning grills now, and when Neilson and MacArdle left, the rush of steam from the passage outside dropped the visibility in the control room to a few feet. Prescott closed the door and moved to Mercer's couch.

"We have a few minutes to spare," he said quietly, as if it was days. "Enough to answer a few questions or to let you get anything off your chest that is bothering you."

Mercer was on the edge of his couch, his legs and arms bent and body poised, ready for a dive toward the door. He was waiting for the fatal thump of the steam explosion aft that would blow the tank's outer seal, fill the ship with superheated vapor, and trap them both in the control room until they boiled in their own body juices. He wanted to kick the First Officer out of the way and escape, right now.

But there was an odd look in Prescott's eyes—a strange one in these circumstances, but familiar. Mercer had seen it on a few occasions when one of his colleagues had become too deeply involved with the suffering of a seriously ill patient. Prescott, he realized suddenly, was *worried* about him. He was inviting

Mercer to bawl him out with no witnesses present, hoping to relieve his fear tensions and to reduce, if only slightly, the panic that was threatening either to paralyze him or send him running to his cabin without any idea of what he was supposed to do when he got there.

Mercer wanted suddenly to laugh, but he got control of himself in time to make it a smile instead. He said, "Permission to go to my cabin, sir?"

Prescott looked relieved as he shook his head and said, "I've been hard on you, Mercer, for two reasons. One is that you have been doing penance for the sins of your predecessor, and the other is that I am hard on everybody. But now you have been dropped in it along with everyone else, and there is time neither to apologize or to tell you exactly what you should do—"

"Eurydice Control. We have looked at your steam jet idea. There is a strong possibility that venting your water astern will check the meltdown and delay detonation for a considerable period. Thought you would like to know."

"Eurydice. Thank you," said Prescott. Then he went on: "So you could do worse than spend the first few days in your couch studying the emergency instructions. An extra complication is that the pods and crew segments will be spinning, or tumbling slowly—because of our control failure the ship power lines were still connected to them and gave, or will give, an off-center tug as they leave. But don't worry about the spin, there is no hurry to correct it. Just try to calm your passengers as quickly as possible, organize your communications, and give them as much help as possible. Good advice is about all you can give them, but don't forget to take some of it yourself. I'll be in touch."

"Good luck, Eurydice."

Without replying, Prescott slid back the door. Hot, choking fog and the blast of a gigantic steam whistle went in as Mercer and Prescott, in that order, went out.

Centrifugal force had changed his sick-bay cabin out of all recognition, Mercer thought as he stood on the transparent canopy gripping two near-vertical bunks. The protective cover had already been released from his canopy, and he could look down past his feet at the apparently motionless and undamaged ship and stars whirling past like a blizzard of jewels. A faint, wavering line held its position in the starry storm—the receding survival pods thrown off minutes earlier. He should talk to them, as soon as he discovered what it was that he was supposed to say.

A few seconds after he had found the emergency instructions booklet there was a series of thuds and clicks, as the cabin went automatically onto internal power and his feet drifted away from the transparent floor.

The stars did not rush past so quickly, but they had a twisting motion which told him that his cabin was no longer spinning evenly with the ship but was tumbling free in the wake of the passenger capsules. He caught a glimpse of another crew segment, the ship whirling past, and the incandescent streak of the Sun.

Mercer checked on the Captain's condition, strapped himself into his couch and tried to read. Outside, the abandoned *Eurydice* was growing smaller each time it whirled past, but he could not see any sign of damage because the Sun dazzled him a split-second later.

He rolled the anti-glare cover across the canopy. If the ship blew, there was no point in risking being blinded by two suns.

Chapter XI

Since only four of the five cabins used by the ship's officers double as survival modules, the Medical Officer and First Officer will share the sick-bay segment, which is fitted with pod frequency radio even more powerful than that carried by the Captain's survival segment. . . .

If he had not been lucky and the Captain unlucky, Mercer would have had to share his segment with Prescott. As things were, the First Officer was now spinning away in the Captain's module.

According to the emergency instructions, the Captain's module contained communications equipment which enabled it to maintain contact with ground control as well as allowing two-way contact with the other officers and, to a limited extent, with passenger pods in its vicinity. There was a frequency which allowed its occupant to listen at any time to what was going on in the other officers' modules, and another chanel which allowed them to call him but not each other. Similarly, the officers had a channel for speaking to the passengers—just one channel, unfortunately, which meant that they had to address all of the pod occupants at once—and another which allowed them to eavesdrop on the pods in case trouble developed among the survivors. But this was also a single channel, which meant that the officer using it would hear all of the passengers who happened to be speaking at any given time.

It was not difficult to understand why the Captain

had to be able to keep close tabs on his officers and a two-way line open to home, or, for that matter, why the sick-bay's radio had most of its power channeled into the pod frequency. The survivors were expected to need medical advice more than any other kind, and with the distance between the potential patients and their doctor increasing every second, advice was all that he could give them.

The sooner he started giving it the better, but he did not want to begin until he understood the problems a little better than did the survivors and could give answers that sounded authoritative.

A large proportion of the manual was devoted to instructions for untrained space officers on how to maneuver and navigate the segment and make the best use of its services and accessories. The instructions for trained astronauts were unnecessarily technical, Mercer thought, while the other set seemed to be aimed at people with a mental age of twelve. The medical side was barely mentioned, whereas the psychological problems he was told to expect seemed incredibly melodramatic. He had to remind himself that even on Earth people managed to do some dramatic things to themselves and each other. When they were spinning through eternity in a ten-foot-wide plastic bubble, driven close to madness by fear and the utter, savage strangeness of it all, it might be easier for them to forget that they were civilized beings.

Suddenly he felt ashamed of himself for lying reading in his couch, with a solid, well-furnished structure around him and the sunlight just a pulsing amber glow behind the canopy filters. He tried to compare his conditions with those on the survival pods, where three or more passengers were tumbling together in a fragile plastic bubble, and he could not readily imagine what it must be like. Some of the passengers might keep their heads and read the very simple instructions printed at intervals on the interior of the plastic film, but it was transparent, and the glare of the unshielded Sun would probably make them impossible to read.

He had been reading for all of twenty-two minutes, by his watch. The technical passages he could study later, but the instructions regarding the passengers should be obeyed as soon as possible. After all, they would not know that he was still reading aloud from the manual.

There was a pullout sheet at the back of the book containing pod numbers and spaces for the names of the occupants. Mercer taped it to the bulkhead beside him and unclipped his mike.

"Your attention, ladies and gentlemen," he said slowly and distinctly. "It is less than half an hour since we abandoned ship. You are probably becoming accustomed to being inside a survival pod by now and are beginning to realize that the accommodation leaves a lot to be desired. However, you are absolutely safe, and the spinning movement of your pods is nothing to worry about.

"Some of you," he went on, "may already have read the instructions for checking spin and have put them into effect. To those who haven't, I shall be able to give instructions for doing so in due course. But first I must check that everyone got safely off the ship. In the confusion there must have been relatives and friends who became separated, and I must begin by making roll-call of all survivors so that I can reassure these people. Would the occupants of Pod One please speak their names, and would everyone else keep absolutely quiet while Pod One is talking."

Mercer flipped up the receiver switch and discovered that everyone was talking at the tops of their voices. He tried again.

"Ladies and gentlemen," he said sharply, "you are all talking at once. I must insist on silence except for the occupants of Pod One."

He became more and more insistent as the minutes slipped past, but he still could not silence the voices from Pods Two through Sixteen. Twice he very nearly had it when only two pods were talking at once, and he almost understood what Pod One was trying so patiently to tell him; but then everyone else seemed to sense that their own personal demands for assistance, advice or information had a chance of being heard, and his speaker poured out only a high-pitched babble.

"All of you, be *quiet!* Pod One, come in, please."

"Pod One. For the fiftieth time, *Mr. Wallace, Mr. Rutherford, Mr. Gunning.*"

"Thank you, One," said Mercer, noting the names on his sheet. "Pod Two?"

"Mrs. Wallace, Mr. Simpson, Mr. McCall. We can't get this damned thing to stop spinning, and the Sun is—"

"Thank you, Two," said Mercer. Relenting slightly, he went on, "Each pod has one pair of anti-glare goggles in its medical pack. Try to remember the pod sequences from the instruction film and let the person with the goggles supervise. I'll come back to you as soon as the tally of passengers is complete. Pod Three?"

"Mrs. Mathewson, Mr. Stone, Mr. Kirk."

"Pod Four?"

"Mr. and Mrs. Corrie."

"Pod Five?"

"Miss Moore, Miss Sampson, Mrs. Kirk and Mr. Eglin."

Mercer made a note to check on the life-support duration of a pod with four occupants, wondering wryly if the psychological problems would turn out to be a much greater threat to the pod's safety than a possible shortage of food and air.

"Pod Six?"

The interruptions were very few, and Mercer worked steadily through his checklist until he came to Pod Eleven, which did not answer. He tried again.

"Pod Eleven, come in please."

Again silence answered him.

Mercer turned up the gain on his receiver to maximum. The silence grew noisier as the sounds of breathing and body movements coming from the other pods were suddenly magnified. Then someone coughed deafeningly, and on Pod Three Mrs. Mathewson thundered, *"Bobby, what's happened to Bobby?"*

He turned down the volume quickly. With nearly three quarters of the pods already reporting in, Mercer had begun to wonder what had happened to the boy, too. But it was by no means certain that he was aboard Eleven. Perhaps there was nobody aboard Eleven.

The ship had carried a more than adequate supply of survival pods for the number of passengers aboard. So far, he had one pod with two people in it, two pods with four people on board, and the rest with three occupants, so it was probable that in the confusion and poor visibility at least one pod had been launched empty.

"Pod Twelve, please."

While he jotted down the names of the passengers on Twelve and then Thirteen, Mercer began to worry in case Eleven's radio was faulty. Where *was* the boy?

"Pod Fourteen?"

"M—Mathewson."

Mercer wanted badly to express his relief, but then he thought about the game he had been playing with young Mathewson, and all at once it seemed to be a good idea, considering what he knew of the boy's background, to go on playing it.

"Very well, Mathewson, please list the names of your crew," he said briskly, and waited.

"Just . . . me."

Mercer wanted to say something, anything, that would reassure the boy, but he needed time to think and he did not have it. All that he could do was go on playing their game, and hope that Bobby would be able to go on playing it as well.

"I copy, Pod Fourteen," he said. "I will come back to you with instructions later, Mathewson. Meanwhile, you have control. Pod Fifteen?"

A few minutes later he had the names of the rest of the survivors and was preparing to check them against the passenger list. The pod frequency was switched off to allow him to concentrate on what he was doing with the small part of his mind that was not worrying about the Mathewson boy, and his mother. During the initial exchange he had repeated back the boy's name simply to let his mother know that he was safe. But now she would know that he was alone as well.

"Prescott. What progress, Mercer?"

Instinctively he reached for the transmit switch to answer, then lowered his hand. Prescott was listening-in in the same way that Mercer was eavesdropping on the passengers. There was nothing he could do about it short of tearing out the radio installation, cutting himself off from everyone else, and risking damage to the other electrical systems in the module. Mercer decided that he did not dislike the sound of Prescott's voice enough to risk any of those things.

"I have completed the tally of survivors," he said, "and now I'm cross-checking against the passenger list."

"Carry on while I talk. The situation at present is that Eurydice *is still pulling ahead of us on her tea-kettle drive, but slowly. Should the reactor go critical now we would have no chance of escaping. But there is a much better chance that it will simply melt into a semi-molten radioactive mess and the resulting mild explosion will scatter debris and radiation over a comparatively small volume of space. This would also mean that the fuel slugs we were carrying as cargo for the Ganymede Base reactor will also be scattered instead of contributing their megatonnage to the blast. Have you got that?"*

"Yes," said Mercer, and added, "All the passengers made it to the pods."

"Good. I spent a few minutes listening to your roll-call. You seem to be handling things fairly well, which is the reason why we are minding our own business and letting you do the same. We have had to spend some time on stabilizing our segments and repositioning them so that our directional antennas will bear—mine on Eurydice Control, Neilson's on the ship in the hope of getting a few minutes warning before she blows, and MacArdle's on the radio beacon we dropped, which will be on low-emission until the time comes for us to burn for rendezvous. I think you were unnecessarily tough on young Mathewson."

Mercer double-checked to make sure that the passengers were not receiving the conversation, but he did not reply.

"I asked a question, Mercer."

"Sorry, I thought you were giving your opinion," said Mercer, not caring if his tone was insubordinate or just angry. "Maybe I was wrong to handle it that way, because I don't know very much about the boy or his mother. But I do know a little.

"The woman is escaping," he went on, his tone becoming more clinical. "Whether from an event or a person I don't at the moment know. I *do* know that the boy's father was far gone on PCs, so perhaps he got himself killed or he suicided during a change party, or maybe he survived physically but with the original personality lost along with the ability to mentate. The woman, I would say, has never been on PCs—she was and is too worried and tense and, well, normal—and the boy shows some signs of emotional disturbance, but is likewise normal. He has a uniform and wants to play spaceman—"

"I noticed that."

"The trouble is," Mercer continued, "I have been playing the game with him by treating him, and talking to him, as if he was a junior ship's officer. Part of the game was that I did not act toward him as I acted toward the other passengers—they were asked to do things, he was told. You realize the position I'm in? If I change suddenly from being a superior officer, even a pretend superior officer, to a sentimental softie who tells him that he is a good boy and not to cry, there could be trouble. His father must have subjected him to the same kind of major personality change several times a week, and the kid did not like it. The way I see it, rather than be nice sometimes and nasty at others, it is better to be consistently nasty."

"I've found that myself."

"The next step," Mercer went on, "will be to help him stabilize his pod and not sound too much like a worried father while I'm doing it."

"Very well, it's your problem."

"And his," said Mercer.

Chapter XII

"Quiet, everyone. Pod Fourteen, come in, please."

Kirk hung close against the interior face of the services module, knees drawn up and elbows tight against his chest as he gripped one of the soft plastic handles which projected from it. Despite the anti-glare goggles he was wearing, he had his eyes tightly shut. His small, hairless head, thick neck, sloping shoulders, and waist which continued to thicken out until it became his hips gave him the visual aspect, from the back, of an enormous, lumpy pear.

Close beside him, Stone was holding on with one hand while the other covered his eyes. "If you're not using the damn things," he whispered, "give them to me."

At the other end of Pod Three, Mrs. Mathewson also had a hand over her eyes. The other one was gripping a screen attachment point, while her head was inclined towards the speaker grill.

"Please," she whispered.

"Sorry," said Stone in an even quieter whisper. "But there are some people who simply take no notice unless you shout at the top of your voice." He tapped Kirk on the shoulder and pointed at the goggles.

Kirk let go of the plastic grip with one hand. Without warning he swung it back, hitting Stone in the chest with his closed fist and forearm and sending him spinning slowly across the pod. Then he pulled off the goggles and threw them after him.

Stone blundered into Mrs. Mathewson's legs and instinctively grabbed them to steady himself, with the result that they both swung into the flexible wall of the
pod, which gave alarmingly with their weight before
bouncing them away again. For a few seconds the
whole pod grew bulges and indentations until it
reached dynamic equilibrium again, and the spinning
Sun took up an even more complex motion.

Squinting against the intermittent glare, Stone fished
the goggles out of the air and put them on. He looked
at Kirk's back for a long time, but the tinted eye-piece
made it impossible to read his expression.

*"I know it isn't. But first you must put on the
goggles. You will find them clipped to the underside of
the lid with a red cross on it. While you are finding
them and putting them on I will explain why this is not
as it was in the demonstration film.*

*"That film showed a simple abandon-ship sequence
which allowed enough time for the pods to be manned
and all ship-to-pod connections severed by the ship's
officers before launching. The connection that has
caused the trouble was a thin cable which carries ship
power to a pod so that it can be tested or used for survival drills without wasting its own internal power.
Usually this cable is cut by a remote-controlled knife,
which is also, for manual operation, fitted to a handle
which projects through the pod hatch cover. But there
was too much steam in the passenger compartment
and not enough time for me to go around pulling
handles, and the circuits to the remote-controlled actuators were dead.*

*"When the pods were launched, the cable, which
goes in at the side of the life-support modules, tugged
the pods sideways as they left and gave some of them a
twist as well. Normally the pods and cabin segments
would not spin at all as they came free, but you have to
remember that there is no real difference between
starting a spin to change the attitude of your vehicle
and stopping it. Just so long as you . . .*

"No, Mathewson, not that kind of knife, but it cuts just as well. Are you ready?"

"It's too complicated," said Mrs. Mathewson.

"He's a smart boy," Stone whispered.

"Right. The first thing to do is to lie as flat as you can against the pod skin, the transparent section, and hold on to the moulded finger-grips in the plastic. Got that? Then move around until the Sun appears to be coming from the top of your head, passing in front of you, and then moving under your feet. Take your time, Mathewson. There's no hurry about this."

Stone stared at the Sun, which was whipping over and around the pod so quickly that he could only guess at its direction of travel. He opened his mouth to speak to Mrs. Mathewson, then remembered that they were supposed to keep the frequency clear for the boy, and shut it again.

Others, apparently, had forgotten.

"Quiet, everyone. I lost some of that, Mathewson. Say again, please, slow and easy."

"Don't cry, Bobby," said Mrs. Mathewson softly. "Please don't cry."

"Going too fast, you say? I see. There is a trick you can try which should beat that one. Get flat against the plastic again, look outside and blink as fast as you can. That will make the Sun seem to stop, or at least to go past in short streaks which will let you know the direction it is traveling in. Ready? Now blink fast . . ."

"It works, by God," breathed Stone.

". . . When you know the direction, get it coming from above your head, going down past your face and under your feet. Keep it moving like that as you start to crawl forward. When you come to the lock section or the services panel, or when you are crawling over plastic which is not transparent, try to keep your line of movement straight by looking ahead to the next transparent section to see where the Sun is. Got that? Then off you go."

Stone began to crawl, trying to keep the incandescent

band of the Sun vertically in front of him and his body flat against the plastic. He was not very successful in doing either.

"I know. But don't try to rush it, Mathewson. Try for a steady even movement and don't worry if the Sun appears to drift sideways—when you have checked the tumbling motion of your vehicle it will be easy for you to turn at right angles and check the sideways movement. But it will be a slow job because this is a solo mission for you. If you had more people on board they could cooperate, space themselves at intervals around the inside of the pod and crawl in the same direction, or hold on to each other with their feet against the plastic and walk sideways.

"But that is their problem, Mathewson. Yours is that your body mass is small in relation to the mass of the vehicle you are controlling, so you are going to have to put in some long-distance crawling."

Stone's erratic crawl took him within a few inches of Kirk. As he moved past he said quietly, "Are you going to help me?"

"I don't know what he's talking about," said Kirk angrily.

"He's explaining," said Stone, "so a ten-year-old would understand it."

"Sorry, Mathewson, your vehicle does not have attitude jets—we don't want to make the job too easy, do we? But you do have some power—two short-duration thrusters, which must be used only to make rendezvous with the recovery ship."

As Stone crawled past Mrs. Mathewson he whispered, "Don't worry, he'll be all right. But I could use some help, and it might take your mind off the boy for a while if you—"

"Stop talking about me, Stone," said Kirk suddenly, "or I'll smash you."

"Quiet! Please keep this frequency clear for Pod Fourteen. That's fine Mathewson—do another circuit on the same line. You won't notice much change until

you've been around twenty or thirty times. If you have any problems, call me. Listening out."

On Pod Three the stabilization exercise was not going well. Stone found it difficult enough to keep his feet and legs from drifting away from the plastic skin, but Mrs. Mathewson was in a worse predicament. She had to cover her eyes with one hand, which made crawling virtually impossible, or use both hands and keep her eyes tightly shut, which meant that she could not see where she was going.

Stone said, "Suppose we stand at opposite sides of the pod with our heads together in the center and facing each other. If we grip each other's arms and begin walking forward, I can guide us while you keep your eyes shut. Would you like to try it for a while?"

But the strain of gripping each other's arms was considerable even if they did not weigh anything, and their combined length was much greater than the internal diameter of the pod, so that the plastic material bulged outwards alarmingly under their feet. But they were beginning to get the hang of it when Stone spoke again.

"I never could stand merry-go-rounds as a kid, you know. Or swings. Especially the instant when you stop swinging up and haven't yet started to come down. This . . . this bothers me. Sometime I'll tell you all about my childish fears, but right now I'm busy. Right foot, Mrs. Mathewson. Now the left, slowly. Right. Left. . . ."

On Pod Five the situation was much less orderly, with four slowly struggling bodies and six plastic screens filling the living space. Just after the pod had been released from the ship the screens had been kicked from their fastenings, and there had been too much shouting and crying since then for anyone to think about re-stowing them. But Mercer's voice on the radio and the Mathewson boy's trouble had brought silence, at least.

"Let's get ourselves organized," whispered Eglin. "We'll start by clearing these crazy mobiles—throw them aft, at me, and I'll re-fold them. Then try to stand with your heads together in the center and your feet at equal intervals around the skin like the man said. I'll wear the goggles and keep you on the right line while you're walking sideways."

Later, as the women were rotating like a human three-bladed propeller, Eglin realized that he could keep them on the right line by watching how the sunlight struck each of them as it whirled around. The effect was visually dramatic, he thought, and he wished that he had had the time to grab his camera.

"Don't rush it, Mathewson. Move slowly and steadily —try to imagine that you are still and that you are pulling the pod around underneath you. Or imagine that you are on the inside of a treadmill. Do you know what a treadmill is?"

Pod Four was already motionless. The opaque, silvered half of its envelope was aimed directly at the Sun, so that the interior was in darkness and the stars shone cold and clear through the transparent section. It was the first pod to be stabilized, and the reason was that Mr. Corrie was an astrophysicist. He had started to check his pod's spin before Mercer had left the control room on *Eurydice.*

"I can see Three and Five," he whispered. "Not very clearly, and in a few hours they will be too far away to see at all. I wish I knew which was which, but I don't know our direction of travel or whether we are right side up with respect to . . . But wait. All the pods are points on the circumference of an expanding circle, so that an imaginary line drawn between Three and Five must pass behind us, so that would give our direction of travel. But I still can't tell whether we're upside down or not. . . ."

"Not so loud, George."

"Sorry, I'd forgotten the boy."

"Do you realize, George," whispered Mrs. Corrie, whose aptitudes had always lain in the softer sciences, "that we've never been really alone together for the past eighteen years?"

"Take another rest, Mathewson. And yes, drink as much and as often as you feel like it. Water will never be a problem, but you don't want to let yourself get overtired or overheated—you can't just open a window, you know. Your life-support system will, in normal conditions, handle the heat generated by three adult bodies at rest, but I may have been working you too hard. While you're resting, read the instructions on the food dispenser and the other essential services. If there is anything you don't understand, ask me."

In Pod Two, Mrs. Wallace was rigging the plastic screens designed to give a measure of privacy to one of the essential services, while Simpson and McCall tried to rotate their now stable vehicle into a position that would give them enough light in which to work without being blinded by the Sun. They were doing this by allowing sunlight to strike the inside face of the entry lock but not to shine into the section enclosed by opaque material.

"Why will water never be a problem?" she asked, and then added, "Oh, I see."

A few minutes later McCall, who was studying the instruction booklet, said, "Water will never be a problem because it is recycled, but to me that implies that there will be other problems—food, air, heat dissipation. It says here that the pod food supply is of a low-residue, highly concentrated kind and that its lack of bulk means we will always feel hungry even though our bodies will have enough to keep them alive. In a three-person pod like this one, the food will last just under two weeks, according to this chart. But everyone knows that it is possible to reduce food intake when they are not using energy. I don't get it. People on lifeboats at sea have survived far longer with less food and a de-salination kit."

"The people on the lifeboats," Simpson said drily, "also had unlimited quantities of fresh air."

"*Quiet, please.*"

Mercer's voice erupted from the pod speakers every few minutes for the next three hours. Sometimes the things he said were immediately helpful to people in difficulties—either physical or psychological—in certain pods. It was as if he had been listening to them, which he was, and had slipped in the answer to their particular problem during his next conversation with the Mathewson boy, which he had. As a result, pod after pod successfully stabilized itself, and the occupants began to rig screens, familiarize themselves with their rather spartan fittings, and generally make themselves as comfortable as possible.

There was no panic. Every time a survivor got excited or even raised his or her voice to an ordinary conversational level, Mercer's voice rattled out of the speaker at them to be quiet and keep the channel clear for Pod Fourteen. It was extremely difficult to have a panic reaction in a whisper, and knowing that someone else was in a worse fix than their own helped quite a lot too.

But finally, even the conversation with Pod Fourteen came to an end.

"*Fine work, Mathewson. Leave rigging your screens until later. Right now you must eat and sleep. That's an order.*

"*You heard that, Mrs. Mathewson—he's all right. You have an astronaut in the family.*"

In Pod Three, Mrs. Mathewson was still holding herself steady with one hand while the other covered her eyes, even though the interior was screened and shaded from the Sun. She was smiling, and large, weightless tears were being squeezed between her fingers.

"*Your attention, ladies and gentlemen. Is there anyone, apart from myself, who has not yet been able to stabilize their pod. . . ?*"

Chapter XIII

"Prescott. What are you doing, Mercer?"

Unlike the uncluttered interior of a survival pod, the medical officer's segment had bunks, an airlock, and cabinets housing various services projecting into it, not to mention the fact that its mass was something like sixteen times that of the passenger vehicles. Checking the module's spin was not an easy matter.

"I'm trying to stabilize the segment," Mercer said, trying also to hide his breathlessness. His legs, arms and shoulders were burning with fatigue, and he wondered if the only thing that was keeping his eyes from dropping shut was the absence of gravity. He added, "Another fifteen minutes should do it."

"Good. While you're working, listen carefully. Mac-Ardle is the worrying kind. He has to compute return courses for each pod and crew segment, which will enable us to make rendezvous should the radio beacon fail. To do this he has to know where, exactly, as well as who, everybody is.

"According to the book, this exercise could be done tomorrow or the next day—even allowing for the increased scatter by that time, the pod flares would be pretty hard to miss. But these people are not trained observers and might miss seeing their neighbors' flares, which means that he could not work out a course for them. He wants that data now. Can you keep young Mathewson awake?"

"The problem there," said Mercer, "is getting him to go to sleep."

"*Right. This is going to take a little time to set up as well as to explain. Listen for the time being, ask for clarification if you don't completely understand something, but go on checking your spin. When you've finished you will need a large sheet of paper and a pencil. . . .*"

It took half an hour for Mercer to get a clear mental picture of what was needed and to explain it all to the passengers. Then he positioned himself close against his canopy with his pod transmitter switched on, his pencil ready, and a large sheet of paper with Prescott's diagram on it taped to the side of a bunk.

The diagram consisted of a circle whose circumference was divided into sixteen equal parts with the points numbered from One to Sixteen in a clockwise direction, which was how the pods had been numbered looking aft from *Eurdice's* control room. Inside this circle was a slightly smaller one representing the positions occupied by the crew segments. The circumference of the second circle was divided into four, but the positions were marked lightly because there was no way of knowing at that time where any particular segment was in relation to any given pod. With luck the next hour or so would give this information.

"*Prescott. Ready when you are, Mercer.*"

"Observations in Pod Two and Sixteen stand by," said Mercer. "Pod One, release your flare."

The distress flares burned brightly for thirty seconds, illuminating an expanding cloud of gas which they released just before ignition, then gradually faded. Neither the expanding circle of pods or the smaller ring of crew segments were sufficiently dispersed for the flares to be invisible because of distance. But Mercer could not see One's flare either in the canopy or through the wide-angle periscope which served the blind areas of his segment.

"*Pod Two. I see it.*"

"Pod Sixteen. Me, too."

"Prescott. I have it."

The First Officer had left on his crew frequency receiver so that Mercer could hear Neilson and Mac-Ardle reporting negative results as well as himself.

"Pods One and Three stand by," he said. "Your turn, Two."

A few seconds later Pod Two was seen by its neighbors and Prescott.

Mercer saw Three's flare bright and clear, and a few minutes later, the flares released by Four and Five. He judged that he was twice as close to Four as he was to Five and marked his position on the inner circle accordingly. At that point he could have marked the positions of the other segments and named them, because they were spaced equally and he knew their order—working clockwise, they were MacArdle, Neilson, Prescott in the Captain's segment, and his own. But he preferred to wait until he heard them reporting in before marking their positions. He acquired Six, and MacArdle and himself were able to see Seven.

Finally it was over. Mercer thanked the passengers for their cooperation, checked the condition of the Captain, and then strapped himself loosely into his couch.

"Prescott. What are you doing now, Mercer?"

"Sleeping," said Mercer.

"Carry on."

Mercer switched off the pod receiver, so that Prescott's voice was the last sound he heard. It was also, after what seemed like only a few minutes, the first. He rubbed his eyes, licked dried lips with a dehydrated tongue, and said, "I'm awake, I think."

"You snore like a shuttle taking off, Mercer. Now listen. I have been doing your job for you—eavesdropping on the survivors—for the last hour. Some of them are beginning to sound worried. But before you start telling them lies, which you are very good at, I want to make sure that your lying and half-truth telling will have a tenuous connection with the real facts of the

situation. I don't want you to be caught in a lie, you understand, because that could be very bad for morale. So, I am a nervous passenger. Reassure me."

"I don't under . . ." began Mercer, then he cleared his throat and said, "What exactly is troubling you, sir?"

"I'll tell you what's troubling me, mister. The smell of this overcrowded goldfish bowl is troubling me. How soon do we get out of it?"

Mercer pulled out his book, then realized that Prescott would probably hear him flipping through the pages, and replaced it. He had a good memory.

"You must realize, sir," he said smoothly, "that all this is largely the product of your mind and its awareness of your crowded conditions, which heightens your sensitivity to perspiration and similar odors. It is not, repeat not, due to any malfunction in your capsule air conditioning or waste disposal or reclamation systems. As for recovery, that should not be delayed by more than a few days—"

"Wrong, Mercer. It could be delayed for more than two weeks."

"Oh," said Mercer. But Prescott was not giving him time to think.

"We're hungry, and it's hot in here."

"You can increase the apparent bulk of the food by adding water, sir. There is no shortage of water."

"We don't like the water. It stinks, too."

"In actual fact, sir, your capsule water, recycled as it is, is much less harmful than that taken from any Earthside reservoir—there is much less pollution in it, for one thing. I'm afraid the smell is purely psychosomatic and comes from you dwelling too much on its source.

"As for the temperature problem," Mercer went on, "that is caused by body heat produced by your recent exertions in getting your pod stabilized and your screens set up. You have probably been moving around and using energy—producing heat—simply because you are excited or curious about your new surroundings. The correct course is to relax and remain absolutely still in the shade of your individual screens, and remove some clothing if you have to until the air-conditioning system brings down the temperature. Drink, and talk, as much as you like, but don't use energy because that produces heat. If you do as I suggest, you will find that the pod temperature will remain comfortable, and even for—"

"Sorry, Mercer. It will get a hell of a lot hotter. Eurydice's course, which is also ours, passes within the orbit of Venus and makes its closest approach to the Sun in nine days time."

Angrily, because he was suddenly so frightened, Mercer said, "What about the recovery ship? Why do we have to wait?"

"I'm supposed to be questioning you. But I'll give you the facts so that you'll know how best to bend them for passenger consumption. The countdown on the recovery ship was started before we abandoned Eurydice, *and at present it is holding at minus twelve hours, which is the time needed to ready the high-acceleration boosters. It is waiting for the same reason that we are, for* Eurydice *to blow."*

"The sooner the better," said Mercer with feeling. "Then we can head back to the rendezvous point."

"Well, no. That might be true if the reactor and cargo radioactives blew up relatively slowly and threw off chunks of slow-moving radioactive debris. We could wait for a day or so until it had cleared the area, and there would be no need to delay launching the recovery ship. But suppose the ship becomes a bomb which flings out a sphere of vaporized metal and generally acts like a scaled-down nova. Close in, this material would go through the capsule plastic like a charge of microscopic buckshot, as well as flooding the area with lethal radiation. At the present time we are much too close to survive it. But the radiation and the effects of the debris diminish with distance. You know about the inverse square law, I suppose?"

"Yes," said Mercer. "The degree of scatter would be

so great that we might not be hit at all, and the radiation danger would be negative. But how long do we have to wait to stand a fair chance of surviving the blowup?"

"A few days. But obviously we can't start back to the rendezvous point until after she blows, otherwise we would be heading into trouble instead of out of it. A complication is that the reactor's fail-safe devices may hold longer than we want them to."

"But the A thrusters in the pods will only accelerate them to sixteen feet per second, which means that they can kill their outward velocity and return at eight, their present outward speed. The operational life of the pods is only two weeks."

"A little more if the occupants do nothing but breathe, sleep and talk without getting excited. You must try to keep them from becoming . . . excited."

"Worried or frightened, you mean?"

"I mean excited."

"Oh."

"Now you will be able to explain to them why the recovery ship will not be launched until after the blowup. Remind them that it is an unmanned, high-acceleration job which will waste no time in getting here.

"There is something else you should do, although there is no great urgency about it. Try to teach the passengers some elementary astronomy. Neilson tells me that, despite the superheated steam which exited from the stern for a few hours after we abandoned ship, Eurydice *has not pulled ahead as quickly as we had hoped. That could mean that the rendezvous beacon might be damaged when she blows and the fancy pod navigation aids, which make re-positioning the pods for the rendezvous burn such an easy job, will not be working. The passengers may then have to take up the proper attitude the hard way, and get it right first time."*

"I understand," said Mercer, wondering where his saliva had gone. He had been too busy until now to have time to feel afraid, and he had thought, in any case, that the worst was over when they escaped safely from *Eurydice*. But the truth was that they had not yet escaped *Eurydice;* and if they did, they might not be able to get back to the pick-up point before their consumables ran out; and there was no absolute guarantee that the recovery ship—which was unmanned and had a long way to come—would make the rendezvous point either.

"That about covers the situation, Mercer. Is there anything else troubling you?"

Mercer was silent for a moment, thinking about his troubles but afraid to start listing them in case he might begin to whine at Prescott. He would rather die than show fear in front of the First Officer, and he wondered, not for the first time, if bravery was simply the stronger fear of being thought a coward.

"Yes, sir," he said finally. "I am a ship's officer needing reassurance. Reassure me."

Chapter XIV

Mercer dispensed a mixture of heavily-shaped truth and quiet optimism, with the result that the passengers, after six days in the survival capsules, were uncomfortable but not unduly worried. A fair proportion of them were unworried enough to feel bored and, despite Mercer's warnings, made attempts to relieve their boredom in fashions which generated a lot of heat.

Pod Four was not the first to generate excessive internal heat, and very probably it would not be the last.

After allowing the higher levels of his mind to be withdrawn from all effective control of his body for several hectic minutes, Corrie was suffering his usual reaction. It took the form of being coldly analytical about everything and everyone around him.

"I cannot understand why it is so hot," he said. "Granted that we are part of a closed and balanced system into which energy in the form of heat has been introduced, there are only two of us in a capsule designed for three, which means that there should be a fifty percent margin on cooling, air supply and food. The second law of thermodynamics states that . . . Let go of me, dear, I want to try an experiment. If I set myself spinning in the middle of the pod, the only energy needed will be that required to initiate the spin, but the movement of air past my skin should have a cooling effect. . . ."

"Don't move," said Mrs. Corrie drowsily.

"But we're hot and slippery and . . . I wonder what it's like on the capsules with three and four people. It must be really hot."

"Not if they behave themselves like the man said, George."

Corrie laughed. He said, "And any minute now our Listening Tom will read us a polite sermon—couched in very general terms, of course, and not mentioning the sinners by name . . ."

"Your attention, ladies and gentlemen. I must remind some of you once again to refrain from unnecessary physical exertion. Rest, conserve your food and air. Exercise should be purely intellectual. I have suggested, and a few of you have devised, some useful question and answer games.

"Mr. Mathewson, it is time for another astronomy lesson. . . ."

It was really hot in Pod Five, almost unbearably hot. But the occupants had no way of knowing how much worse were the conditions in Five than in the pods carrying the Corries or the threesome of Stone, Kirk and Mrs. Mathewson, so they just complained as everyone else was complaining. Some of the complaints went unvoiced—the stench produced by perspiration, the overloaded waste disposal unit, and the equally overworked water reclamation system—because they were trying very hard not to think about those particular problems.

In Five, the plastic screens which had shielded the occupants from each other had been dismantled when it was discovered that they interfered with the free circulation of the air. The removal of the screens generated a lot of emotional heat, while making the environment fractionally cooler. Surprisingly, the removal of other items which interfered with the free circulation of air, such as clothing, was accomplished with very little fuss. It had become much too hot to worry about clothing, or the neo-Puritanism which dictated that the female body be completely covered except in the privacy of the home. Perhaps Pod Five was beginning to feel like home.

"I'm hot and hungry," said Mrs. Kirk suddenly. "I've read about people being cold and hungry. I envy them."

"And I envy you," said Miss Moore, who was spinning slowly about her longitudinal axis, legs and arms akimbo and even her fingers open to catch the maximum benefits from her self-generated breeze. She went on, "I envy your flab. You've got more fatty reserves than the rest of us put together, and an enforced diet is just what you need. By rights you shouldn't eat anything, because we will starve long before you do, especially if we go on splitting the food four ways. I'm hungry, too, damn you."

"It isn't nice to call me flabby, even if it is true," said Mrs. Kirk. "Besides, my husband is even fatter than I am, and he must be suffering terribly by now. Fat people have enlarged stomachs, you know, and feel much hungrier than slim ones like you. But you are just afraid of being so thin that Eglin will stop ogling you."

"I want out of this thing," said Miss Sampson. She was drifting close against the transparent section, staring into space. "Please, can I get out of this thing?"

"Don't be stupid," said Miss Moore without taking her eyes off Mrs. Kirk. "Your pigmentation gives you protection against the heat, and you people are born and raised in famine conditions."

"I think you're wrong," said Mrs. Kirk. "Their skin color protects them against strong sunlight, but not against high humidity. I remember reading that—"

"Reading must have been your only form of amusement," said Miss Moore, "and looking at you I can understand why."

"That isn't—"

"I can remember reading a story," Miss Moore went on, "where the oldest and most expendable member of a party of travelers was sacrificed for the safety of the others. They threw her to the wolves, as I remember. We would not be so wasteful. What do you say, Sampson? Cannibalism was practiced by your people fairly recently. Give us the benefit of your expertise."

"Soap, a bathe," said Miss Sampson. "A swim in the sea."

"I don't blame her for ignoring you," said Mrs. Kirk. She paused for a moment, and when she went on her voice was quiet, reasonable, and utterly malicious. "Seriously, you would never get hungry enough to eat me because you haven't really thought about what it would entail. Not all of me is edible, you know, and the waste disposal unit will take just so much. Bones, for instance. Some of them would be big and hard to break up into a convenient size for the unit—especially when they are freshly gnawed and slippery and you can only use your teeth and bare hands to break them. And then there are items like hair and toe-nails and lungs and eye-balls and—"

"You're making me sick."

"If you are as hungry as you say," said Mrs. Kirk, "I don't see how you can have anything to be sick with."

"Shut up," said Eglin, "both of you."

For a few moments there was silence, although the atmosphere was thickly charged with anger in addition to the heat, humidity, and a multiplicity of body odors. Eglin could not help noticing the atmosphere because his lips were pressed together in anger and he was breathing heavily through his nose as he glared at the three of them in turn.

During the first few days in the pod, Eglin had been too embarrassed to even look at them when they were fully clothed, because he usually found that they were looking at him, and he did not know what they were thinking when he looked at them, or what they thought he might be thinking when he looked at them. And when the increasing heat and humidity forced them all to peel, it had been even more embarrassing, but only for a short time, because very often he was in fact thinking what they thought he was thinking, and there was no way for him to conceal the fact. So he had begun staring at each of them in turn, so that their feelings would not be hurt by his appearing to admire one of them more than the others.

Now he was too hot and angry and frustrated and hungry to bother showing consideration, and he spent most of the time watching Miss Moore because she was the best looking one, and she usually caused the most trouble.

Eglin ran his hand over his forehead, face, and the wet, black smear that was his week-old beard, pushing away the thick, weightless drops of sweat. He thought of several ways of making Miss Moore stop her continuous arguing and sniping and blatant displaying of her undoubtedly beautiful body, all of them pleasant—to him. He was so engrossed that the trouble was already started before he realized that there was any danger at all.

Miss Sampson was sobbing and clawing furiously at the plastic envelope, and her nails were long because, unlike the other two, she did not nibble at them when she was worried. When the fury of her attack caused her to drift away from the plastic, she kicked at it, which sent her bouncing against the opposite side, where she clawed and kicked again. With each bounce the fabric of the pod stretched and bulged frighteningly, and the Sun bobbed over the edge of the opaque section. Several times she collided with Miss Moore and Mrs. Kirk, but accidentally, because she did not try to attack them. At least, not until Mrs. Kirk tried to restrain her and got two long, red nail-marks on her forearm for her trouble.

Cursing, Eglin planted his feet against the solid plastic of the services panel and launched himself on an interception course They collided softly and awkwardly, rolling and bouncing along the plastic canopy until they ended in the middle of the pod, spinning slowly together.

By that time Eglin was facing her and had a tight grip on both her wrists, holding them against the small of her back. He was afraid for a moment that she might use her knees on him, or take a bite out of his face with her even and startlingly white teeth, but suddenly she relaxed against him and began to cry.

"Nice try, Sampson," said Miss Moore furiously. "Hysterics, a good old-fashioned wrestle, and then the dissolve into tears—the oldest trick there is. But it isn't going to get you anything, Sampson, because it's too damned hot in here as it is. Get *away* from him!"

"Jealous?" asked Mrs. Kirk.

But they were each gripping one of Miss Sampson's shoulders and pushing Eglin away with their free hands. He realized, not for the first time since they had been flung away from *Eurydice* together, that he was living in a wish-fulfilment dream but that, for all the good it was doing him, he might just as well be living in a monastery.

"All right, all right," he said in a tone which said it most decidedly was not all right. "If you can't sleep and won't stop nagging at each other, let's do what the man says and try a little intellectual exercise— guessing games." He flung out an arm in an angry wave that encompassed the pod, the people in it, and the whole of creation outside, and said, "I'm thinking of something beginning with . . . with S."

"Saggitarius," said Mrs. Kirk.

"The . . . the Sun," said Miss Sampson.

"Obviously," said Miss Moore.

"If you can't see the constellations as I've described them, don't change the attitude of your pod. Spin yourself very slowly inside the transparent section and watch the stars until you see the proper formation. That way uses less energy and produces much less heat."

In Pod Three, the situation was somewhat different.

A hypothetical observer armed with a very accurate thermometer would have said that the internal temperature was fractionally cooler than that of Pod Five. A psychiatrist would have been worried sick.

Kirk drifted like some lumpy, organic airship over the services panel, permanently tethered to it by one fat, hairy hand. His eyes never seemed to leave Mrs. Mathewson, who floated at the other end of the pod. The only times he did not watch her was when Stone managed to drift between them, which was as often as possible.

There were no guessing games, no quizzes, no group intellectual exercises of any kind in Pod Three. When Kirk spoke, he broke a silence which had lasted for six hours.

"Why does he talk to the kid so much?" he complained. "The boy is a special case, I know, but Mercer could surely give someone else the benefit of his individual attention. There is more than one survivor, you know."

It was a reasonable complaint compared with some of the others he had made earlier, and his tone was conciliatory—as if he were trying to start a conversation which would not end in a bitter argument. Mrs. Mathewson brushed away the hair that was clinging wetly to her face and said, "I think he's trying to teach and help all of us, as Mr. Stone said, and is pretending to teach only Bobby so as not to offend the others by making it too simple for them."

She looked from one man to the other, trying to bring them together and pleading silently with Stone not to make things worse. But Stone was not looking at her and so could not hear the silent pleading.

"You're cheating on the food, Kirk," he said. "We aren't getting our fair share."

"You don't need a fair share," said the other man. "A skinny runt like you needs to eat hardly anything."

"I've always wanted to try a crash diet," said Mrs.

Mathewson, still trying to pour on some verbal oil, "and never had the nerve. But now—"

"Inside every fat man," said Stone, still not looking at her, "there is a skinny slob who let himself go."

"Please," said Mrs. Mathewson, "please stop fighting over the food."

Stone drifted slowly around to face her. He said, "Use your brain, woman. We're not fighting over the food."

"Your attention, ladies and gentlemen. As you know, we are following Eurydice's *original course, which during the next few days will make its closest approach to the Sun. Let me assure you that the temperature will not rise above bearable limits, even in the pods which are overcrowded, provided you remain at rest and do not generate unnecessary heat. The food supply is adequate; it is simply that its lack of bulk makes you think that you are starving, and the elevated temperature is also causing a rapid loss of weight.*

"Think of the situation like this. Taken as a whole, the Earth is also overcrowded and underfed, and firm control is needed if the available resources are not to be wasted and the population is not to perish of its own pollution or by too much self-generated atomic heat. You people are all facing the same problems on a greatly reduced scale, and some of you are having to adapt to situations which rarely, if ever, occur on Earth —social imbalance, conflict, a small-scale war may even seem to be unavoidable. But a war will kill everyone in your tiny plastic world just as surely as it would decimate your home planet. You must avoid fighting at all costs.

"Remember that you are human beings and not animals, and keep control."

In Pod Fourteen control was easy, if slow. Mathewson knew exactly how to change the attitude of his vehicle, and he was learning how to line up the dividing line between the clear and the opaque material with groups of stars when Mercer gave the order. He was hungry, but not very, and he was not uncomfortably warm even with his uniform and cap on. Fourteen's life-support system, catering as it was for one young boy instead of three adults, was keeping him comfortable.

Mercer had given him permission to strip if he wanted to, but had warned him against exposing his skin to the Sun. That way he could get a very serious and uncomfortable burn. According to Mercer, the only space-tanned astronauts were the ones who appeared in TV plays. Real spacemen avoided the Sun, and if one of them got burned, it was a mark of sheer carelessness. A good spaceman learned to control himself as well as his ship, Mercer had said, and keep his mind busy and alert. Space was a very beautiful, but a very lonely and dangerous place, if one did not keep control.

Mathewson knew that he did not always keep control. Sometimes he wanted to play some other game than this one of Spaceman, which never stopped. At such times he tired of memorizing stars and doing practice runs over the tiny control panel, or crawling inch by inch along the plastic to keep a certain star exactly in position. But he could not change the game, and he couldn't even stop playing it.

Sometimes he wondered if Mercer knew when he lost control and started shouting to fill up the emptiness, or crying because there was nobody near him. After he had cried the first time, Mercer had explained to someone in another pod that there were psychological and technical reasons why he could not arrange two-way contact with separated husbands and wives and loved ones. He had said that arguments within the pods were hard enough to control without risking them starting between the capsules, and also, the passengers were becoming so widely scattered that his receiver's speaker could not be turned up loud enough to energize his transmitter mike, which was on a bulkhead several feet away.

But Mercer could not have heard him crying because he had not changed—he had not called him a good boy or praised him or talked soppy. Mercer had started by treating him like one of the crew and had not changed at all, so he must have been busy at something else when Mathewson was crying or shouting. As the commander of this spacecraft, he should not be caught crying, and he should stop doing it before his luck ran out and Mercer caught him at it.

But sometimes when he awoke with no bed or blankets around him, just warm air and plastic and very faraway stars, he got frightened and couldn't help it because he wanted his mother.

"Attention, attention. I have received a signal that Eurydice *will blow in approximately three minutes. Whatever you are doing, cover your eyes at once. Keep them covered for at least thirty seconds after the flash. Do not, I repeat, do not try to watch it through your goggles or peak at it between a crack in your fingers.*

"If you look it could be the last thing you will ever see."

While he was speaking, Mercer pushed the Captain's bunk into its recess and shut the airtight flap. Between the metal of the bunk, the bandages, and the damaged eyes, which might not be capable of registering light anyway, Collingwood was adequately protected from the flash. Mercer covered his face as he had told the passengers to do because Prescott had told him to do it, but in much more pungent language.

Despite his hand and his tightly closed eyes behind it, he saw the flash as a bright, pink blotch which faded very slowly.

When he uncovered to look outside he saw a beautiful, spherical aurora writhing and expanding to fill all of space. The radio brought in a deafening rattle of static, and the radiation level was climbing steadily.

While he had been relaying Neilson's warning, Prescott had said that the reactor's safety devices had kept

the cork in too long and that it would be a big one—
possibly the biggest nuclear explosion so far—but they
should be safe. Mercer hoped that the First Officer
was not simply trying to be reassuring.

Chapter XV

Through the window of Brannigan's office the recovery ship stood against the sky like a narrow white pyramid wrapped in the red lace of its service gantries. There were no signs of activity on or around it, but that situation could be changed within a few minutes. The decision would be his alone, and he should take it now instead of pretending that it would be arrived at by the democratic process of listening to advice. Brannigan swung away from the window to stare along the center of the table which joined his desk like the vertical bar of a fat, grey T.

To nobody in particular he said, "We're wasting time."

"I disagree," said Perkins. "It is less than thirty-five minutes since *Eurydice* blew."

"That bird out there costs nearly twice as much as the lost ship," said Musgrave; then he added apologetically, "As the company accountant I'm supposed to remind you of things like that before you throw good money after bad."

"He has a point," said Beck. "The delayed blowup will not hurt anyone, but a lot more delay will be caused while making sure that untrained passengers point themselves properly at the rendezvous point, plus, of course, the time needed to get there. I can place that bird within one thousand meters of their rendezvous beacon, but will there be anyone there to rescue? We really should wait until we have their report on the consumables."

"We might wait a long time," said McKeever in his dry, lecturing voice. "The blast has converted *Eurydice* into a rapidly expanding zone of radio interference—rather like a spherical Heaviside Layer—through which we, with our high-powered equipment, can punch a signal. But they don't have the power to answer us until the volume of interference has enlarged and become so diffuse that their signal and that of rendezvous beacon, if it still exists, can get through.

"The shortest estimate that I can give for the clearance of this radio fog is three days," McKeever went on, "and it seems to me that Beck cannot simply aim at the center of the explosion because Neilson used a crude steam jet, whose angle and thrust are not known with accuracy, which caused *Eurydice* to move ahead and probably veer off course. If we are going for a late-evening launch we will have to use the figures MacArdle gave us."

"But can we accept them for a launch as important as this?" asked Beck. "And if the beacon has been taken out by the explosion, how will the passengers find their way to the rendezvous point anyway?"

Dr. Lassiter cleared his throat. He said, "With one exception, I know these officers very well indeed. You can accept MacArdle's figures. As for the passengers making rendezvous without a beacon, you know that the medic has been giving simple lessons in astrology and astro-navigation—coached by Prescott and MacArdle, of course."

"Do you approve of Mercer?" asked Beck. "Does Prescott?"

"I do," said Lassiter, "and Prescott approves of nothing and nobody. But he hasn't called Mercer incompetent, which is tantamount to an unsolicited testimonial. The part that worries me, however, is the fact that the pods will arrive at the rendezvous point dangerously low on air, and the two overloaded capsules in an even worse condition. That ship out there is fast, but we've had to wait a long time while *Eurydice* made up her mind to blow, and the survivors are very far away now. My figures aren't as accurate as Beck's, but I'd say that if we don't launch as soon as possible there will be an awful lot of freshly-asphyxiated corpses at the rendezvous point."

Dr. Lassiter represented the softest science in the room, which was why he tended to worry more about the space-going software.

"That's it," said Brannigan abruptly. "We try for a rescue."

With the decision taken—apparently by democratic process—Beck communicated it to the launch crew. Any remaining questions would be those of policy, and where policy was concerned, Brannigan was a dictator.

"If we go for a rescue," said Westgate suddenly, "we will have to say a lot more about the disaster. What do I tell the media?"

"Nothing," said Brannigan. "The first major accident has occurred to a passenger-carrying spaceship, the passengers and ship's officers are safe in their survival capsules, and a rescue operation already formulated to meet this contingency has been put into effect. Nothing more until we know whether or not it is successful."

Westgate's objections were smooth as a good PR man's should be, and not immediately identifiable as objections. He said, "Yes, of course. There have been no fatalities as yet, and there is no reason to worry the next-of-kin until they actually occur. At the same time, we are going to be held responsible for this disaster by the public, even though we can show that it was a vendor company who was really to blame. Unless we focus a lot of unwelcome attention elsewhere for a while—long enough for us to work out satisfactory answers to a number of very awkward questions—we could take an awful pasting from the press and TV.

Those boys hate like hell to have anything kept from them.

"This is the first disaster of its kind," Westgate went on, "and it has everything. The Captain injured, perhaps dying, and unable to direct the survival operation. One pod with a kid in it trying to do the job of three men. The conditions inside the pods while they were waiting for *Eurydice* to blow, the heat and hunger and overcrowding, the strangers thrown together into conditions of intimacy, and the imbalance sex-wise. It is the biggest cliff-hanger since Apollo Thirteen. There would be no problem in slanting it to make us look like heroes instead of villains, and to handle it so that the majority of the media people will feel obligated to us for life. . . ."

The others joined in, arguing with Westgate and putting up alternative suggestions. Everyone seemed to have the idea that public relations, like writing, photography and painting, was a job that could be performed just as well by amateurs. Doctor Lassiter sat staring silently into the far distance at fragile plastic bubbles full of hot, stale and stinking air, and thinking of the people who were being forced to breathe it. Brannigan was staring into the same area of space.

"Checking sequence initiated on booster rings Two, Three and Four," said a voice from the speaker on Brannigan's desk. *"Checks completed on tanks A and B on ring One and fueling under way. Minus eleven hours and thirty-seven minutes, and counting. . . ."*

Everything looked so normal and peaceful, Mercer thought resentfully as he tried to dry the perspiration from his face with even wetter hands. The vaporized plastic and metal that had been the ship had cooled and scattered into invisibility, and only the deafening rattle of static on the pod frequency was left—that and the radiation indicator, which was rapidly slipping back to normal.

He had turned down the volume on the pod fre-

quency because the voices he heard were either lost in
the mush or were all talking at once. So as not to feel
completely useless, he spent some time helping the Captain, stripping him of all but his bandages to make him
feel as comfortable as possible, and reinforcing his sedation. Then he drifted back to the canopy to think and
sweat and look at the stars.

Static erupted thunderously from his speaker, with a
whisper of intelligence trying to fight its way through
the din. Mercer gritted his teeth and moved closer.

"*Prescott. Come in, Mercer.*"

"Mercer here. Go ahead."

"*Prescott. Come in, Mercer. Try to . . . against the
mike and . . . be able to hear you.*"

Mercer put his lips within an inch of the mike and
acknowledged at the top of his voice.

"*Better. Now listen carefully and . . . for a repeat if
you don't . . . MacArdle says that this muck will clear
over the next few . . . will allow pod and segment
frequencies to be worked in about two hours, but two-
way contact with* Eurydice *Control will not be possible
for at least . . . But they know what to do without me
telling them. Our job is to get the pods headed back
. . . possible after the segments are on their way, I will
link you to . . . your instructions.*

"*In case you're thinking that it's wrong . . . passengers should go first. We must . . . rendezvous first to
help look for them . . . on stragglers. If you understand . . . to MacArdle.*"

"I understand," Mercer shouted, and a new voice
began fighting its way through the interference.

"*MacArdle. The Beacon was taken out by the blowup so . . . the hard way. Your A thrusters are set
below the floor-grill center line. When you fire make
. . . you are diametrically opposite . . . occupied by the
Captain so that . . . weights will be equally distributed
about your center of thrust. Have you got that?*"

"Yes," bellowed Mercer.

"*You won't be able to see the sky in your direction*

*of thrust because of the segment configuration, and
neither will the pod people because their services module will be in the way, so you will have to establish
attitude from points at right angles to your proposed
line of flight. You will . . . sitting position with your
back to the seal and sight along the top edge of the
third line of bunks. The glare-shield supports will give
you a second referent and . . . lower half of Orion
projects from the right into your canopy field of view
just above the center line. Below . . . Sirius on the opposite edge of the canopy and, although you won't be
able to see it from that position, if you lean to the left
you will have Aldebaran and above it the Pleiades as a
check. Do . . . repeat that?"*

"No."

*"You understand . . . a first approximation and that
. . . more accurate attitude checks later. Is there any
other information you need?"*

"No, thanks," yelled Mercer, and added, "you seem
to have a photographic memory where my segment is
concerned. Were you a patient in it?"

*"Detailed structural data . . . in the Captain's seg-
ment. Prescott worked out the sighting arrangements.
But now you must get your segment lined up with . . .
me know when you're ready for the first attitude check."*

"I'll give you a shout."

"That's very good, Doctor."

*"Prescott. Stop chattering, you two. MacArdle, Neil-
son next. Mercer, you know what you have to do."*

While Mercer sweated at changing the attitude of his
segment he could not help looking at the locked control
panel set above his couch. Like the other crew segments,
there was provision for making rapid and accurate
changes of attitude, but anyone who was not a trained
astronaut could very easily send his vehicle spinning
helplessly out of control if he tried using anything but
the pre-measured A and B thrusters. Prescott had not
even mentioned the possibility of his being able to fly
the vehicle, much less forbidden him to do so.

The radio interference had faded a little as he worked. When Mercer turned up the volume on the pod frequency he could make out a babble of voices through the static. Apparently they were now close to the center of the expanding sphere of interference, and signals could get neither in nor out. But the sphere was hollow, and the people inside it could talk to each other and would be able to do so with less and less trouble as time went on.

He heard every word that MacArdle spoke while he made the tiny movements which placed the segment into its pre-burn position. He held himself still as instructed, making sure that the segment was not drifting off the line. But when MacArdle spoke again he could not move at all, and for several minutes he could not even speak.

"MacArdle. Acknowledge, Mercer. Have you got trouble?"

He could actually feel the globules of sweat growing on his skin, making his hands slippery and his back skid along the lock seal. He shook his head violently, and the newly-dislodged perspiration drifted before his face and tasted salty when he breathed it in. The stars burning coldly though the canopy were suddenly a mass of incomprehensible lights with no recognizable order or meaning, the imaginary lines which linked them together gone, so that he did not know what he was seeing.

Mercer had thought that he could not feel more afraid than he had in the howling, steam-filled chaos of the passenger compartment of *Eurydice,* but he had been wrong.

"I . . . I don't think I've got this right," he said finally.

There was a silence which stretched for an eternity, but which could only have lasted a few seconds. Mercer wondered if MacArdle would speak, or if Prescott would cut in with some pointed and abrasive comment.

He could just imagine what the First Officer was thinking about him now.

"MacArdle. You seemed to be doing fine until a few minutes ago—I mean, the Pleiades and Sirius and Orion are pretty distinctive referents. But just try to relax, drift forward to the canopy, and have a good look around to make absolutely sure that you have the right constellations. Make sure you shield your eyes from the Sun or you'll waste a lot of time waiting for your night vision to come back. But take your time. Don't let me rush you, and don't push the button because you're afraid or ashamed or because you want to put yourself out of your agony. You must get it right first time."

Mercer's voice wouldn't work.

"Maybe the Captain can help you."

"The Captain is under sedation," said Mercer sharply, "and he can't see, anyway. I would only be giving him something more to worry about. I'll go forward and have another look around."

"I was going to ask you to do that in any case, Doctor. We all have to double-check on something as important as this. And remember, when you start your burn give me a ten-second countdown so that I will know the exact time of firing and the time you will have to fire your B thrusters at the rendezvous point— otherwise you might go sailing past. And don't worry if there seems to be nobody there when you arrive— we may be too widely scattered to see each other without flares."

When the burn came, the sensation of weight was so strange that Mercer thought he would drown in the softness of the bunk. In a few seconds it was over, and he coiled and stowed the cable and remote-control switch, which had enabled him to fire the thruster from his position opposite the Captain.

"Prescott. The sooner the pods are turned around the better, Mercer. You have done most of the talking to

them so far, and you may as well continue. How will you handle it? Numerically?"

"Yes," said Mercer. "Taking them in numerical order will stop any argument about who gets their instructions first—but there are exceptions. Two of the pods are carrying four people and will run out of air before the others, one of the threes is a potentially explosive situation, one may have a leak, and nobody will object to the Mathewson boy jumping the queue—"

"I do, Mercer. Bringing back the pods that are in hazard first is a good idea, but the boy can comfortably wait his turn, or even come in last. He will not, repeat not, run out of air and food."

"I understand," said Mercer.

"Good. Now go to work on the passengers. Don't waste time, but don't appear to be rushing them, either. MacArdle will give you the referents for each pod as you need them, and you will translate them to your passengers. I, ah, know that you will appreciate their problems."

Chapter XVI

"One of us," said Stone, "is considerably heavier than the other two. Will this swing us off course when we apply thrust?"

"*Not very much, Three, but you may as well get it absolutely right and seat the two lighter passengers closer together and facing the heavy one. But make sure that your movements have not set up a drift away from your marker stars.*"

"You never miss a trick," muttered Kirk.

"Don't be so blasted sensitive," returned Stone. "I deliberately did not say which of us was the fat one, and I very much doubt if Mercer remembers us. Relax, Kirk—it was a purely technical question. Or is the thought of me sitting close to the lady bothering you?"

"Don't tell me to relax in that tone of voice," said Kirk angrily. "You're deliberately giving Mercer the impression that I'm ready to go berserk and that all I can think about is women."

"You certainly haven't thought much about repositioning this thing," Stone replied. "And don't *move* or we'll have to spend another half-hour getting the right stars lined up. Be a good man and wait until after the burn before you take a swipe at me."

"I didn't have to think about it, with a cool scientific mind like yours directing the operation," Kirk said. "Or maybe you are just pretending to know it all so that she will think you are some kind of scientist champion who deserves, and intends to claim, his prize—"

"Shut up, Kirk."

"In a minute. I just want to remind you of a scientific fact. This overweight body which you are always making cracks about, and which *she* tries not to look at, has lived on Earth for fifty-two years. It has developed muscles to lift and move itself around under one Earth gravity—pretty big muscles, though they don't show—and in weightless conditions they will not be hampered very much by the fatty overlay. Just remember that before you start claiming any prizes."

"Stop it," said Mrs. Mathewson, speaking for the first time that day. "Stop fighting, and stop talking about me as if I was one of the food packs. You're both old enough to have more sense. Besides, the lucky winner could not claim his prize—if he tried we would all die of heatstroke."

"Attention, Pod Three. Are you stable and ready for thrust? Do you want to recheck your attitude?"

"We have rechecked our attitude four times," said Stone, glaring at Kirk, "and we're as stable as we're ever going to be. And anybody with half a brain knows that if we haven't got it right, then we've no hope of reaching the—"

"Relax, Stone," said Kirk nastily.

"We're firing . . . now," said Stone.

"Thank you, Three. I shall pass you the repositioning information in plenty of time for you to fire the braking thrusters at rendezvous. Pod Four, come in, please. . . ."

The operation was smooth and fast on Pod Four, because Corrie had been listening to Mercer's instructions to the other capsules and had already worked out a close approximation of his pod's firing attitude, so that only a few minutes spent on minor corrections were needed to position it accurately. The relationship between Mercer and the astrophysicist during the exchange of information was that of a pupil and a rather irascible teacher—and Mercer wasn't the teacher. Corrie did most of the talking until the moment when he pushed the thrust button and his wife made a sound that would have been a scream if she had not been breathing in at the time, and pointed.

"Don't wave your arm about, dear," said Corrie, "or you will cause a deviation in course. But I see what you mean."

"Having trouble, Four?"

"Just an unpleasant surprise," Corrie replied. "When we applied thrust the sidewalls bulged outwards and the lock-section forward looked for a moment as if it would come down on our heads. Actually, it approached by only a few feet, and now that thrust has ceased, it and the sidewalls have returned to normal. But you might have warned us that this would happen. That was inconsiderate of you, Mercer."

Corrie waited for more than a minute, then said testily, "Mercer, did you hear me?"

"I hear you, Four. Sorry about that. Was there any indication of a swing off course when it happened?"

"No deviation," said Corrie.

"Good. Thank you, Four. Pod Five, come in."

As Corrie drifted away from the services panel, he wondered if he had detected a note of strain in Mercer's voice. He was becoming very familiar with the sound of the medical officer's voice because, like the occupants of all the other survival capsules, it was the only outside sound that they heard. He wondered why Mercer had waited before answering him. Was Mercer irritated because a passenger had made a legitimate complaint at a time when he was very busy? Was he feeling as hot and uncomfortable as was Corrie, and panting in the stinking, humid air as if he had just run a mile? Or was it simply that Mercer had been talking so long, repeating the same instructions over and over again, that he was going hoarse?

But there was no way of escaping Mercer's voice, so

Corrie panted and sweated and listened to the medic being patient with the stupid ones, and reassuring with the frightened ones, and both at the same time with the majority of them. The only consolation was that Mercer seemed to be speeding up the process—while one pod was lining itself up on its marker stars, he had taken to giving the next two pods their attitude instructions.

He ran into a slow patch between Pods Ten and Thirteen because the Sun occupied the sky close to their markers on one side and the passenger wearing the goggles could not see the stars clearly, while the others dazzled themselves trying and had to wait until their night vision returned. Mercer's voice was very loud during this period, probably because the pods concerned were at extreme range for his radio.

Corrie wondered why the other officers were not helping him, but then decided that Mercer's radio was probably designed for this kind of work, and that it was his duty to look after the survivors while the other supermen did what they had to do about organizing the recovery. He had not spoken to any of the other officers, and had seen two of them only briefly, but he recognized the type. They were the kind of men who were tops at their job—highly trained and even more highly intelligent misfits who did not communicate easily with normal people.

Corrie understood them very well because he was that kind of person himself, a refugee in a do-it-yourself ivory tower.

Possibly the injured Captain had been less aloof. Corrie had heard a few words which Mercer had not intended the passengers to hear before the medic had remembered to switch off, so he knew that Collingwood was unfit for duty. Which was a pity, because Collingwood, judging by the way he had chatted with the passengers as they were coming aboard, might have been able to mix socially during the voyage. Or it might be that the crew were not allowed to have anything to do with the passengers—especially female passengers—in the interests of discipline.

Except for the ship's medical officer, that is, who had acted like a glorified steward and not at all like a superman until the disaster had occurred. He could imagine the feelings of the other officers toward the one who had free access, professionally and otherwise, to the passengers. They must have been knotted up with envy, with people like the Moore girl undulating about the ship. Or did they sympathize with him instead, looking down on him from their control room monastery as a kind of worker-priest whose duties placed him in the greatest danger of all, that of being blackballed out of the club if he made a slip?

"Pod Fourteen, come in, Mathewson. Twelve and Thirteen will need a little time to check their attitudes, and you may need even more because of your small mass. I shall read your marker stars so that you can start lining up your vehicle now and save time when I come back to you for the final checks. Ready to copy?"

Corrie cursed the heat, and the air that would not stay in his lungs for more than a second, but not loudly enough to interfere with the conversation going on between Mercer and the boy. When he was physically or mentally uncomfortable he had a tendency to lash out at people or, if they were not within lashing distance, to think nasty thoughts about them.

It was quite possible that Mercer was passing on instructions from a book. The medic's treatment of the boy was, on the surface, completely unsympathetic. But Corrie knew that he was judging the situation by only one half of a conversation. If he could hear the other half, he would know how thoughtless Mercer was being towards the boy, or otherwise. Certainly there was no indication, in the half which he could hear, that the boy was frightened or hysterical or unable to handle the job properly. Perhaps Mercer's half of the conversation was simply a ruse to fool the boy's mother into thinking that everything was going well with her son. Maybe the majority of the instructions to the passengers were like that; maybe most of the pods had actually been unable to take up their proper pre-burn attitude and would never reach the rendezvous point. Not everyone was as well-informed as Corrie, after all, and even he could not be absolutely sure that he had done the job properly.

Corrie tried to bend his mind onto a more pleasant line of thought, an almost impossible task with Mercer's voice dinning in his ear every few minutes. If he could not close his ears, at least he could look out of this hot, stinking hell at the cold, clear beauty of the stars. But the transparent plastic was smeared with condensation in several places—the first time he had known that to happen—and the only heavenly body he could see clearly was that of his wife.

Viewed objectively, it was not a heavenly body in any sense of the word, but then Corrie had been unable to regard it objectively in the thirty years he had known it. In the beginning, when it had been rounded and firm and very much younger, he had loved it so much that it had been impossible to feel any objectivity about it, and when the years began to pass and the structure changed and thickened as it adapted to the changes brought about by childbirth, he had not wanted to be objective. Neither could he be objective when the muscle tone began to diminish and his heavenly body had begun to sag and wrinkle and grow lined under the triple forces of age, gravity, and grief.

He thought of their daughter on the way to that dance, impaled like a beautiful butterfly on the steering column of her car—and decided that it was much more pleasant to think about his wife and their present predicament. He had gone after, and gained, a very important post on Ganymede Base so that his wife would be able, if not to forget, at least not to be constantly reminded by well-meaning friends of the tragedy. She would keep herself busy teaching in a technologically advanced village school with a dome over it, and the prospect had already made her begin to relax. The absence of gravity had smoothed out a lot of her wrinkles as well, and she was certainly looking much better than she had for years.

Corrie reached out to touch her, then stopped. It was not simply that putting his hot, moist hand on her would be uncomfortable for her and cut down the area of evaporation; there had always been this hesitancy about the first touch, the initial invasion of privacy. From the very beginning there had been this shyness about wanting each other and an awkwardness about expressing their feelings—as if some hypothetical listener would make scathing remarks if they called each other by pet names. And so what had started as a joke to cover his shyness had gradually become for them the language of love.

Like a dedicated astronomer taking up a lifelong study specialty, he had made a close study of his heavenly body until he knew it thoroughly inside and out, knew its powers of attraction and the serious perturbations it caused when, as frequently happened, it made a very close approach and variations of the two-body problem had to be worked out. But no matter what he did, or how coldly scientific was his language at the time, the result was invariably the same—two close binaries going nova together with the release of considerable energy and heat.

"Heat," he whispered angrily, "is the newest four-letter word."

She opened her eyes and saw his hand a few inches from her face. Suddenly she gripped it and pulled him towards her. They bounced softly together, and she wrapped her arms tightly around his back before she spoke.

"I'm hot and sticky and not nice for you," she whispered between gasps for breath. "I'm bothering you and it isn't fair, but I'm afraid. I can't breathe, George. I'm . . . I think I'm going to die."

"Don't cry," Corrie whispered, smiling, "you'll increase the humidity. And you aren't bothering me—it's too damned hot to be bothered."

"It isn't a joke," she said, desperation making her speak the first few words aloud. "I'm suffocating. Every time I breathe out I don't know if I'll be able to breathe in again. I can't stand it. My head is bursting and . . . and I'm drowning in here. I'm going to die, George."

"No you won't," said Corrie quietly. "Try to think of something pleasant, like that time I stuffed the snowball down your neck. The heat is bad, but the suffocating sensation is all in your mind. We have plenty of air, remember—think of what it must be like in a pod with three or four people in it."

He broke off, gasping for breath and with big black splotches jerking across his field of vision. It had been too much to say in one breath, but he had tried to do it because it had seemed the best way of proving to her that they were not short of air.

A little later he went on, "Mercer has been talking to Pod Sixteen and nobody else for the past twenty minutes, so he will soon be finished. When he stops talking we can get some sleep. Try to relax. We have nothing to worry about and plenty of air."

"Thank you, Sixteen. That completes the exercise, ladies and gentlemen. We shall meet again at the rendezvous area in approximately six and a half days."

We hope, thought Corrie, then went on aloud, "Why don't you shut up and go to sleep?"

"That was good advice, whoever it was who gave it. I agree; all of you try to sleep. With one exception. Come in, Pod Four."

Startled, Corrie said, "Pod Four."

"We have been considering the incident—the only one of its kind to be reported—which you mentioned during retro fire, when your pod became uniformly de-

formed while thrust was being applied. We think you have a problem, Four."

"We are pretty sure that you have been punctured by one or more small particles of the ship and that you have suffered a drastic, but obviously not lethal, pressure drop. The drop has been so gradual that you may have attributed your difficulty in breathing to the heat, but the sooner you repair the leak, or leaks, the better.

"You will find a tube of sealing compound, clearly marked, in a recess in the services panel. If you can't read or understand the instructions for any reason—anoxia, impairment of vision, anything like that—ask me. Otherwise do not waste time or oxygen acknowledging my instructions.

"The punctures in the transparent section of your pod will appear as patches of condensation. Closer examination will show that they are actually small clouds of water vapor boiling off into space. Punctures in the opaque area will be harder to find. Use empty food tubes, torn open and flattened. Cover the opaque area systematically, using the opened tubes. The tube plastic is thin and will stick to any point where air is escaping.

"Don't try to take a shortcut by covering a larger area with a piece torn from a plastic screen. You could easily miss a leak that way, and the screen plastic is tough—you must avoid wasting energy when the oxygen level is low or you will pass out. Work carefully and thoroughly and with minimum effort. If you haven't asphyxiated already, there should be ample time to plug the leaks before you do, and then, of course, you won't."

Corrie was busy long before Mercer had finished talking, and he did not have to ask for clarification or further instructions. He spoke only briefly to give directions to his wife, and although they used minimum effort on the job, they completed it feeling that they had been boiled in their own body fluids. Corrie looked at their handiwork—six small blobs of sealing compound

where three tiny pieces of *Eurydice* had come and gone
—and wondered what it would have been like to have
been hit by one of those tiny, radioactive bullets. One
of them, if he remembered his position correctly when
the explosion had occurred, must have passed within
inches of his head.

"Pod Four," he said. "Finished."

*"Thank you, Four. Pressure will come up fairly
quickly now, but I'm afraid the news isn't all good. You
have lost a lot of air and no longer have the fifty percent safety margin which you started with. If you'll
pardon the expression, you are in the same boat as the
other, three-passenger pods. But don't worry about it.
Rest and sleep as much as possible. That goes for
everyone."*

Corrie drifted, eyes closed and feeling fractionally
more comfortable than he had been for days, thinking
about Mercer. The medic had known for hours that
Pod Four was leaking air—the pause when Corrie had
complained about the sudden flexibility of the walls
during thrust had been Mercer reporting to the other
officers, no doubt. But he had not mentioned it to
Corrie until the very end, after the pods carrying four
and then three people had been turned around—the
pods that would reach the rendezvous very short of air
indeed. If they got out of this, Corrie did not know
whether he should compliment Mercer or punch his
face.

"The next time you tell me you're dying, dear," he
said, "I'll believe you."

The voice of Mercer kept him from hearing his wife's
reply.

*"Your attention, ladies and gentlemen. The radio in-
terference caused by the ship blowup is beginning to
fade, and we have had a signal from* Eurydice *Control.
The recovery ship took off three hours ago; it is on
course and estimating the pick-up point in a little over
a week. Now I'm going to sleep."*

Chapter XVII

He was monitoring the pod frequency with the volume turned down, and all he could hear was the faint hiss of interference and, very occasionally, a very quiet voice complaining about the heat, the smell, the hunger, or the other people in the pod. If something happened in the survival capsules which needed his attention, the quality and tone of the voices would change enough to worry his subconscious into waking him up. Mercer had never felt so tired in all the thirty-two years of his life.

But his fatigue was mental rather than physical—the only muscles that he had used had been those controlling his tongue—and his brain did not have enough sense to go to sleep easily. He had to go through it compartment by compartment, switching off, powering down, forbidding it to worry or feel guilty or responsible for situations and people over which he had very little influence and no direct control. And he, too, had to try to forget the heat and the hunger, when it was within his power to ease both conditions where he personally was concerned.

Prescott, without actually forbidding him to use the individual air-conditioning systems and stores for the bunks, had reminded him that he would need to save as much power and consumables as possible for the transfer of passengers to the recovery ship.

He tried not to worry about what might happen at the rendezvous—if his segment reached it, or if the recov-

136

ery ship reached it. There was nothing he could do for the Captain, either—Collingwood's treatment was palliative rather than curative. He could be of no real help to the passengers, either, except as an eavesdropper who could head off a panic or potential fight by giving the offending parties something else to think about. They were simply names and voices to him, for the most part, because apart from the Mathewsons, Stone, and Miss Moore, there had not been enough time to fix everyone in his memory as individuals.

As Mercer drifted loosely above his couch, with the soporific hiss of interference and the occasional murmuring of passengers' voices reinforcing the humming of his own life-support equipment, it became increasingly difficult to separate the real sounds from the ones he dreamed, and almost impossible to tell them apart when his dreams began to use real sound effects. But he could recognize the voices, even when they were slurred with fatigue, distorted by anger, or segmented and separated by long, gasping pauses for breath.

Dreamlike, the remembered voice of Prescott built itself up from the background noises, telling him that the passengers could not possibly be as short of air as they sounded—not even the ones who were four to a pod—and that the gaspings were due to unnecessary exertion, heat, and thinking too much about a shortage of air that had not happened yet. That, of course, was before Mercer had reported the deformation of Pod Four during thrust and Prescott had decided that the Corries' shortage of breath was actual rather than imagined.

Mercer had wanted to tell Four's occupants as soon as possible about their trouble. Prescott had objected, saying that doing so would unsettle the passengers who had not been turned around by delaying their retro fire and making them wonder if their own pods were not just a little bit soft. Telling the Corries too soon could quite easily have brought on another six emergencies just like theirs. When Mercer had continued to argue,

Prescott had ended by asking him to wake the Captain for a second opinion.

"No," said Mercer, because the Captain, dressed only in sweat-soaked bandages, was feeling his way around the segment. Where Collingwood's spacesuit had not pressed tightly against his skin, the decompression had caused capillary bleeding and the blood had congealed, so that his face and neck were like one great, livid bruise, and the same angry discoloration marched along his body and limbs in broad, regular bands. He kept looking straight at Mercer with his eye bandages and smiling and asking for a report and offering to help.

Mercer said "No" again, because it did not much matter what he said to the Captain in a dream. He told Collingwood that he could do nothing to help if he could not see, because Mercer's greatest fear was that he had misdirected the segment so that they would never make rendezvous, and that the Captain's instructions and those of Prescott would probably be in conflict. In any case, the Captain was a patient, and doctors were not supposed to worry patients with their physician's personal troubles when they had plenty of their own.

The Captain replied that he was dying from radiation poisoning even though neither of them would admit it while they were awake, that he was so full of sedatives that he was walking in someone else's sleep, and didn't Mercer want company? Mercer insisted that the Captain would worsen even his dream condition by moving around and talking, and that the radioactive material he had inhaled could easily be dislodged and start burning another area of lung tissue.

But the Captain remained hanging there, talking politely and refusing to return to the bunk, which he could not possibly have escaped from in the first place. Mercer wondered if he could dream him back into the bunk, or if he would have to dream himself awake and push

Collingwood into the thing. But if he dreamed himself awake he might really wake up.

Mercer did not want to wake for as long as possible. Sleep was infinitely precious—it short-circuited a few of the boring, anxious, sweating hours of waiting for rendezvous and rescue, or for the realization to come that he was off-course, with no hope of rescue. He would allow the Captain in his dream provided Collingwood did not become too unpleasant—it would be a small enough price to pay for sleep. But he could not help wishing that his dream did not take over where his waking life left off.

Gradually, Collingwood's intent, bandaged face began to fade away, as did the bunks and the segment structure behind it, and Mercer was hanging in emptiness, rendered even more empty by the crowding stars. Voices were coming out of the emptiness from a ring of tiny plastic globes, which hung like effluviant bubbles in a black ocean.

"I can't. You know I never could sleep properly without you beside me—no, George, you're too hot. Just . . . just hold my hand until I'm asleep."

"Your tiny hand is sweating, let me—"

"You can't sing, George, and you're wasting oxygen."

"I agree," murmured Mercer, "on both counts." .

"It's supposed to be cold and dark, they told us. But this . . . it's like a black inferno. I keep wanting to tear a hole in the plastic and climb out—it would be worth asphyxiating just to be cool for a few seconds."

"Take it easy, Sampson. If you did that you wouldn't even have time to feel cool. You would decompress, swell up and burst like a balloon stuffed with porridge. You wouldn't look or feel nice at all."

"And you only have to look at Kirk herself to see what she means about overstuffed—"

"There's no need for cracks like that, Moore—I was simply trying to keep her from killing herself and us into the bargain. But maybe you would like to die, too,

because you have nothing left to live for. Even when you nudge against Eglin he just pushes you away now. You must be getting desperate. Your cheek-bones stick out, and as for your gorgeous figure, we can count every rib. You're skinny, Moore, and you can't take it. That's the trouble with beautiful and unstable creatures who live only for love—"

"Listen, Fatso, an overweight hog like you has no reason to talk about psychological instability. You're not exactly an attractive sight yourself. You've three times more skin than you need, and it flaps around like a—"

"You bitch. You can't leave me alone, can you? Well, just remember that three can live and breathe more easily than four, and the next time you're drifting about trying to nudge Eglin and you come near me, I'll—"

"Shut up, all of you! You're wasting air, and even getting angry generates physical heat, so cut out the squabbling, ladies. If you want to do things, lie quiet and think about doing them when we get back on the recovery ship, where there will be enough food and cool, clean air to let us do them without killing ourselves, right? If you think about it quietly, you will let me go to sleep and dream about it. You might even go to sleep yourselves. As for you, miss, I don't really believe that you would tear a hole in the skin, but your long nails worry me. Why don't you chew them like I do. It's a good way of augmenting your diet."

"Sensible man," said Mercer. "Always leave them laughing." He wondered sleepily if biting the nails was in itself a mild form of cannibalism.

"Eh-eh-eh-eh-eh-eh. Whi-i-n-n-g-g-g. Blam-blam-blam, Kerpow. Eh-eh-eh- bo-o-om. Charge!"

The Mathewson boy's capsule was having another war. It did not sound like Indians this time, or bug-eyed monsters—arrows, Mercer knew from recent experience, went whizz-thunk, and ray-guns simply hissed. This sounded like a group of assault commandos of

Second World War vintage in the process of establishing a bridgehead on Pod Fourteen. Mercer did not object either to the noise or the occupation, because it was much better than listening to the boy trying not to cry for his mother, and the visitors were not using up any of the food or oxygen. Besides, a battle of this magnitude would soon make him hoarse, and the imaginative effort involved would put him to sleep.

"He hasn't spoken for over four hours. Do you think our radio has packed up?"

"You worry too much, Saddler. He's probably sleeping. After all, he's only human."

"You don't really believe that, do you? I wonder where they found such a cold, unflappable, unemotional iceberg for a medical officer—"

"Poker, anyone? Whist?"

"We just finished a game. Can't you think of anything else, like what it would be like if we had a girl in here?"

"We might not be able to do anything. I mean, that's a game that only two should play."

"Not always. It has been practiced as a group exercise on occasions."

"No dice, Saddler—Mercer would deliver a sermon, much stronger than the one he gave somebody three days ago, warning us about abusing the energy reserves of our restricted worlds in the thoughtless pursuit of pleasure, and the doll herself would probably remind us that she had a husband—seven feet tall and broad in proportion—in another pod."

"But nobody could actually stop us, could they? I'm thinking about that paragraph on page twenty-three of the emergency instructions where it says, in effect, that any actions taken by survivors while adrift in a capsule are beyond the jurisdiction of any planetary government. We could get away with anything."

"Like cheating at cards?"

"Don't be ridiculous; some sins are unforgivable. But he might be right, Saddler—we could be luckier than

some of the others. A pack of cards doesn't use oxygen, and if things get really bad we can always eat them."

"Gin rummy, then?"

"Try patience," said Mercer in his sleep. "That's the name of this game."

"I don't dislike either of you. Try to believe that and stop arguing over what I probably think about you— I'm thinking none of those things. It doesn't make any difference to me that one of you is fat and the other thin, even less that one is polite and apparently thoughtful while the other is less so. I'm a PC widow with a wide experience of being loved, hated, tolerated or ignored by a man who changed personalities at will. The only good thing about you two, so far as I'm concerned, is that neither of you change."

"That might not always hold true, m'am. In the grip of strong emotion, such as love, even the most stable personality can undergo—"

"Say what you mean, Stone. Given the chance, you would be as much an animal as any other man."

"That kind of personality change is normal in those circumstances and doesn't worry me."

"I should think not. My wife wouldn't complain if I came home a different man every night. What happened to him? Was he institutionalized, or did he get airborne without a airplane?"

"Shut up, Kirk."

"It doesn't matter. You probably think it was fun. It was, in the beginning; then he took PC only occasionally, when he had to meet an important client and he thought it would help him swing the deal if he put on a complimentary personality. But then he started taking them more and more often, and experimenting, and for the last four years his personality was so fragmented that it made him impotent. But he kept taking more, several different kinds at once, trying to shock his mind back to normal. They told him that it didn't work like that, but he wouldn't believe them. That was how

*he died. At a party, after taking five, one of which was
a hallucinogen—it was that kind of party. But he didn't
commit suicide. Three of them got impatient to experience the drug under free-fall conditions. They were
holding on to each other all the way to the pavement."*

"Tough."

"Yes, indeed."

*"It doesn't bother me now. But you see why I don't
like or dislike either of you, and why it is a waste of
time fighting over me. Nothing could happen here anyway, but perhaps if I came to know both of you better
on the ship—"*

*"Stone might get to know you better on the ship, but
I wouldn't—my wife would be there. And I'm not all
that sure that we'll ever make the ship. That sanctimonious medic is conning us, and you are likely to be
the last woman I will ever meet. My personality isn't
very nice, but I'm likely to be the last man you will ever
meet. For obvious reasons I'm discounting Stone, who
probably couldn't—"*

*"Kirk, you're trying to start a fight again, and you'll
get it—on the recovery ship if I can wait that long—"*

"Please. Please don't fight. . ."

"MacArdle," said Mercer urgently. "Neilson. Prescott. Wake up, MacArdle, and listen to me. I have to
try something but I need your help. . . ." He went on
calling the Communications Officer, outlining what he
had to do and asking for instructions. But MacArdle did
not answer, and all he could see was the survival pod
with Mrs. Mathewson and Stone in it, with a great organic zeppelin without a face, which was Kirk. But then
the picture began to fade, and the supports of the bunk
beside him began to show through. Something, somebody, was waking him up, and he was actually glad.

*". . . And if you insist on babbling in your sleep, at
least talk coherently! Mercer! Prescott here, come in,
Mercer."*

"Mercer."

"I think I caught the general drift, but tell me again what you want MacArdle to do, and why."

Mercer began by explaining that he still wasn't sure whether he had overheard some pod conversations or merely dreamed that he had, and when Prescott curtly informed him that he had overheard the same conversations, his tone became even more demanding. Without giving Prescott a chance to speak again, he concluded, ". . . I've been listening to them and understand the type of personalities involved. With that background of PC trouble with her husband, she can't help feeling the way she does; but the other two should not, in those conditions, be told that she has no strong feelings either way for them. If she said that she preferred one, fine— they might have a token scrap and some bad language. They might even injure each other proving who was the better man. But telling them that they are just the same in her eyes—well, they have both got to prove to her as well as themselves that they are not the same, and before they do I have to get over there and stop it. . . ."

"Negative. Absolutely not. The segments and pods are all, we hope, heading for rendezvous. Making course corrections to bring your segment alongside Three is a much too complex operation at this stage."

"But MacArdle had the return courses ready as soon as we needed them. He must have a computer that could easily—"

"You've got one just like it, Mercer, but you've spent your life programming it with medical data. The answer is no."

"But they'll kill each other."

"Talk them out of it, Mercer. There is nothing else you can do."

Chapter XVIII

His trouble was that he could not talk to the passengers as individuals, even though, on many occasions during the days which followed, he was sorely tempted to do so.

On Pod Three, it was Mrs. Mathewson who did most of the talking, as she, too, tried desperately to keep the peace. He learned an awful lot about her from the things she said—about the life she had so recently led, the pressures she had been under, and the difficulties of bringing up her son in a home that was all too often a madhouse. Other survivors revealed things good and bad about themselves, but Mercer's interest in them and his concern for their welfare was professional—Mrs. Mathewson and her boy he was beginning to like. If he wasn't very careful, he could find himself acquiring a ready-made family.

It was a ridiculous, if pleasant, thought, which seemed to come to mind much more often when he was asleep than awake, and on some of those occasions he was able to do much more than talk to Kirk and Stone. One of the first things he usually did was to forget his Hippocratic Oath, lose his temper, and begin making medical repair work for himself.

He had to remind himself that they were three reasonably normal, civilized people, who would not have dreamed of hurting each other in ordinary circumstances, and that he had better keep reminding them of that as often as possible.

The trouble was that he could not talk to them directly, although it could be done very easily by calling for silence from everyone else and talking frankly about their situation. But then he would remember that while the frank discussion was going on between the occupants of Pod Three and himself, everyone else would be listening to his half of the discussion—including the Mathewson boy and Kirk's wife. Mercer did not want the boy to hear the sort of things Kirk was saying to his mother, even at second hand, and open discussion might easily be the cause of violence in Pod Five as well. The trouble in Pod Three, like a virulent disease, had to be contained.

So he talked to Three in general terms, telling cautionary tales, drawing comparisons between pod conditions and those on the overcrowded Earth, stressing the importance of self-control and the necessity for eking out the available resources for as long as possible. When the reactions from the pods—not just from Three—told him that he was beginning to anger them with his preaching, he changed his approach and began talking psychology, discussing the well-known fact that individual members of certain species, when threatened with death or a lesser danger, sometimes displayed a tendency to seek to prolong their lives through their offspring, either by protecting them against the danger or by seeking to produce more of them. This urge toward species immortality was an animal instinct which reasoning beings could easily overcome.

From that he moved to debating. More accurately, he answered at length questions that had never been asked. The survivors could not hear anything but his side of the debate, so they did not know who asked the questions Mercer was answering, and when some of them asked good questions of their own, he sometimes tried to answer those, too. But when the questions were difficult or potentially unsettling, he pretended that too many people were talking at once and that he had not heard them.

He knew from their reactions that most of them knew he was getting at someone, and speculation regarding the identity of the unknown offenders was rife and served to keep their minds off the heat and hunger for several days. In Pod Three they knew who Mercer was getting at, but Kirk and Stone had stopped talking, or even cursing at him, and Mrs. Mathewson seemed to realize that nothing he could say at a distance of several hundred miles would be able to help her.

That made two of them.

"Some of the passengers consider me a nuisance," he told Prescott during his next report, "others a constant irritant and a bore, while most of them show active dislike. But on Pod Three . . .Well, everything I say now, on whatever subject, makes them angry with me and each other—the men that is. There's going to be bloody murder in that pod if someone doesn't make them see sense. Do you think you, as the most senior officer, could talk to them and—"

"I know I couldn't, Mercer. Nor could Neilson or MacArdle—we aren't programmed for that sort of thing. How is the Captain?"

"Still out. If I allowed him to regain full consciousness he would be confused—I'd have to explain everything that has happened in detail to him—and in considerable pain. It would not be fair to him, and he might not be sufficiently well to sound authoritive enough to quell the people in Three. But then I can't, either, and the reactions of the other passengers—"

"Are you worried by what they think of you, Mercer? Don't be. I've listened to some of the things they've called you—several varieties of sanctimonious unprintable, a blasted nag where conservation is concerned, a cold-blooded, imperturbable zombie who apparently can't even treat a boy with kindness. But why go on. I'm beginning to feel proud of you, Mercer."

"Thank you, I think."

"However, I can help by giving your people something else to think about. MacArdle has computed the

attitudes for the rendezvous retro burn, but it will involve you giving the passengers another lecture. I'll give you the positions, marker stars and firing times in numerical order, beginning with your own, which will be first. Are you ready to copy?"

"Ready," said Mercer.

"Before I give you the data, explain to them—in your words, not mine—that for this burn the attitude is not as important as the timing. They must check their velocity as close as possible to the rendezvous point. If they make a small error in attitude, it will cause only a correspondingly small lateral drift, and we will be able to keep them in sight and pick them up when the recovery ship arrives—that is, of course, assuming they have not made a major attitude error which will take them wide of the recovery area. If they burn their B thrusters too soon or too late, they will stop short or overshoot, and we may not be able to find them without the recovery ship's radar, and by then their air could be gone. Do you want me to repeat this?"

"No."

"The first burn, yours, will take place in a little over five hours. The two four-person pods will follow, then the remainder in numerical order, with the last few having nearly a day to practice their positioning maneuvers. With luck, a fair number of pods will be converging towards visual contact shortly, which should also give your people something pleasant to think about.

"Your burn will occur at twenty-two zero six, and your marker stars are . . ."

During the hours that passed before Mercer had to make his burn, the reactions from the pods ran the gamut from wild excitement to the listlessness of utter despair. But morale improved considerably when Pods Ten and Twelve reported seeing another pod, which meant that they were seeing each other. Mercer did not tell them that to see each other so soon meant that one or the other was considerably off course.

When the time came for him to apply thrust he had not seen anyone else, even though the other three crew segments had reported seeing each other and should have been within easy visual range of him. Mercer tried to consider the possibility that he was off course, lost, and for a few minutes so great was his panic that he could not even think. But then he began to feel angry as well as afraid, angry with MacArdle for giving him such precise instructions when, if Mercer had not carried out the repositioning properly a week earlier, this present exercise was a sheer waste of time. He surprised himself by making the final attitude check and pressing the thrust button precisely on the pip.

But when he moved to the canopy to make another desperate search of the stars for the three segments, the fear returned. He wondered again if he should rouse the Captain, if it would be fair to wake Collingwood only to explain that, due to an error on Mercer's part, they were lost and were going to die. It might not be fair, but was it right? Did anyone have the right to put a man to sleep, then make the condition permanent without first waking him to tell him so? Maybe he would hate Mercer for waking him, but perhaps there were things that Collingwood wanted to remember for a while before he died. There was that startlingly beautiful ground hostess who was the Captain's wife, possibly children, other experiences and people. . . .

"Where the hell are you?" Mercer shouted.

"Prescott. Steady, Mercer. We could ask the same of you. Try lighting a flare."

Keeping his eyes covered to retain his night vision, Mercer ejected a flare, not daring to hope.

"We have you, Mercer. MacArdle says that from your position we should be midway between Triangulum and the Square of Pegasus, in visual range now that you know where to look. Well?"

"I see you," said Mercer after a few minutes. With thousands of stars all around him, the arrival of three small and not particularly bright additions had not been easy to detect. "Can I get closer?"

"Yes, by using your flares for thrust. You ignite them without pressing the eject button. This causes them to burn inside their launcher, giving ten seconds of very weak thrust. But it isn't necessary to come closer. We can expect some pretty wild shooting from the passengers and having you out there to look for stragglers could be an advantage, and the recovery ship might come to rest closer to you than us."

"I understand."

"It's nice seeing you, Mercer. Now you had better attend to Pod Five."

On Pod Five, Eglin had passed out from heatstroke, and the three girls had positioned the capsule and applied thrust. Mercer did not see their burn, nor those of Pods One and Two, but they were spotted by the other segments and he relayed the good news to their occupants. Several passengers reported excitedly that they could see other pods, and Mercer spotted one drifting almost directly between himself and the dim constellation of artificial stars that was the other three crew segments. He did not know who it was until its B thruster burned outwards like a fiery spear precisely on the second listed for Pod Three.

"I see you, Three," said Mercer, almost laughing with relief. "Nice shooting."

"Stone here. I'm not just a pretty face, you know. But this little miracle of astrogation is going to cost someone, Mercer."

"Fine," said Mercer, laughing. "Company rules forbid the carrying of intoxicating liquor, but if you wouldn't mind a few ounces of diluted surgical spirit, I'd be glad to——"

"He doesn't want to be paid off in hooch, stupid."

"That was Kirk, Mercer. Ignore him; he isn't responsible for his glands."

"Don't you patronize me, you . . . you gentleman——"

"Please don't fight. We're nearly safe now. Please. Doctor, talk to them."

There was nothing that Mercer could say that would do any good, so he said nothing. There was very little that he could do, but he did it.

"Prescott. Are you in trouble, Mercer? There is evidence of a discharge of gas from your vehicle."

"No, sir. I used two contained flares to move towards Pod Three—"

"I told you to stay put."

"Yes, sir. But a very serious problem could arise on Three if something isn't done quickly, and it is in my province. I guessed that you might object, and I decided that it would be better—less prejudicial to discipline, that is—if I were to be chewed out for using my initiative rather than for disobeying orders."

"That was considerate of you, Mercer. I suppose you consider mutiny just another exercise of individual initiative? Don't answer, I'm too busy just now to listen. Neilson will tell you what to do if you ever get where you're going."

Before Prescott switched off, Mercer could hear Mac-Ardle reading out the numbers for what he called his final approximation of position, while another voice, sibilant with distance and intervening interference, was reminding Prescott that the survival pods were nearing their limit of duration and suggesting ways by which the passengers could save energy and air. The voice from Earth was speaking as if it was surrounded by mikes and TV cameras, which was probably the case, and Mercer hoped that Prescott would give the ground-bound medic instructions on what to do with his elementary and unoriginal suggestions.

The flares had not given his segment much of a push, so that it would take five hours for him to reach Pod Three—if he did not go wide. He had three flares left, two for deceleration and one to light if he got lost. It was extremely difficult to listen to the sounds from Pod Three without thinking too much about what might be happening there, but he tried. The voices from the other pods helped.

"*Pod Four; Corrie, at rest. I have two others in sight.*"

"*I can see someone! Pod Six here. Shouldn't we decelerate now?*"

"*Pod Seven. We can see a pod on a converging course. Who is it?*"

"*Mercer, the air is bad. When I look at the stars I keep seeing blotches. I'm not sure if they're the right ones.*"

"*Pod Five. Sampson. The others have passed out and . . . and I'm going the same way. The air indicator is as . . . as near zero as makes no difference. Where the . . . hell's the . . . recovery ship?*"

"*Prescott. I heard that, Mercer. Tell her there is a safety reserve and to relax. Make it sound convincing. I'm going after them myself, estimating contact in five and a half hours. Is there anything special I should remember about reviving heatstroke and asphyxiation cases?*"

"*I can't breathe, George.*"

"*Crowded all of a sudden, isn't it? I can see three of them, all drifting past us. It's like . . . Oh God, no. We're moving past them; we're going right past them. Saddler here. What's happening to us. . . ?*"

"*Prescott. I see them, Mercer. Their attitude was badly off—they killed only a fraction of their inwards velocity and are shooting away from the rendezvous area at a fair clip. MacArdle, go after them before they get too far away. Mercer, tell them to relax and play some more poker.*"

"*Pod Fourteen; Mathewson. When will I be able to see something, Mercer?*"

"*Pod Nine here. We're due to decelerate soon but we still can't see anyone. Are . . . are we lost?*"

"*I don't think that I'm the sort of man he keeps telling you I am—I'm pretty sure I'm not. But I don't know for sure, and I don't want to hurt you. Even*

*under this blubber I'm a big man, you know, and
. . . Well, you've heard of the expression 'laugh and
grow fat.' I think that fat people have to laugh to keep
from crying or breaking things, and small people keep
jumping about and prodding people so's everyone will
know they're there. . . ."*

"Watch it, Kirk."

". . . in noise what they lack in size. But they're
lucky in some ways. They are better engineered, less
susceptible to component failure like bad hearts and
gummed-up arteries, and there are always plenty of
small, good-looking women for them. Unless you've
plenty of money or you put on weight after you're
married, nobody will look at you but fat women. Just
once, before I die, I would like to be loved by a beautiful slim girl with a nice disposition and . . . Well you
know."

"I understand, Mr. Kirk. But we aren't going to die
and that wasn't, well, isn't, how I'd describe myself. I'm
a bag of skin and bones."

"Ignore him, m'am. On you, skin and bones look
good."

"Damn you, Stone. You always have to say the right
thing."

"Kirk, what are you doing. . . ?"

The fight started then, and Mercer would not reach
them for another three and a half hours.

Chapter XIX

He began by telling himself that it could not possibly last, that they could not maintain the physical effort in an environment of a stinking plastic oven full of rank air—but the fight went on and on with no audible indication of it ever stopping. Then he began to worry about the heat they were generating and the air they were using. Reminding himself that both men were suffering from malnutrition and could well be as weak as kittens did not help much, because the noises they were making suggested that they were fighting like tigers. What they were doing was a physical impossibility for sane men, and insanity like this had to be temporary.

But temporary did not necessarily mean of short duration.

The grunts and gasps, the low, monotonous cursing, and the wet thud of fists or feet against slippery, sweating flesh went on. Mercer told himself that his imagination was probably working overtime, that they were not seriously injuring each other because in the weightless condition it was practically impossible to kick or punch accurately and, if a blow should land, both attacker and victim would bounce away unless they were holding each other tightly—and if they were doing that they would not be able to punch or kick effectively.

There was a sudden high, sharp squeal of pain.

"*Stop it! Stop it! Look what you've done to his ear. . . .*"

Animal noises answered her. Probably they were

154

making them at each other. But there were other times when the noises became coherent words, when, between the curses and grunts of pain, they became all too specific about what they were going to do—what they *were* doing—to each other. So there were very few blank areas in the mental picture that Mercer had of the interior of Three, and those were usually filled by the anguished pleading of Mrs. Mathewson trying to keep the two men from killing each other, and her as well.

"*It's getting hotter! Stop it. Please stop it. . . .*"

Mercer heard another wet thud and a feminine cry, as Mrs. Mathewson tried vainly to separate them; then another scream, followed by a continuous whimpering and moaning, as one of the men sank his teeth into the other's shoulder and had his eye clawed while he was tearing free. Mercer knew what was happening because they kept talking and gloating about it, but he did not know who was doing what because neither of the men's voices was recognizable.

Mercer had forgotten that in the weightless condition they could still use fingers and teeth.

"*Pod Ten. I'm having trouble again finding my markers. Is Arcturus supposed to be level with the rod equator and Antares ten degrees above it, or have I got it the wrong way around?*"

"You have fifty minutes before your burn, Ten," said Mercer sharply. "I'll come back to you. Quiet, everyone, for Pod Three."

"*Prescott. Forget Three, Mercer, and think about your other passengers. Give Ten the information he needs. Right now.*"

"But those two are killing each other, and probably the girl, too. Listen to them."

"*I'm trying not to, Mercer. I advise you to do the same.*"

He could not forget Pod Three because the sounds on the capsule frequency kept reminding him that the biting and clawing and gouging were still going on. But suddenly there was a marked reduction in the noise and activity—maybe the heat was getting to them at last and they were beginning to flag. With luck they might both pass out from heatstroke, which meant that they would stop using so much of the pod's air and all of the occupants' might survive, even if two of them did not deserve to.

There was just over two hours to go before he rendezvoused with Three, if he was able to do so, and there might just be enough air for them to make it.

"You've won, you've won. Let go of him. Can't you see you're strangling him?"

"I've won. No. And yes."

"But . . . but you're not angry any more and you're still trying to kill him. Let go. Let go of his throat."

"Keep off. I'll wrestle with you later. . . ."

"Let go of him. Please let go . . . Oh, my hair, my hair. . . ."

"I told you to keep off. . . ."

Listening helplessly, Mercer knew that things were quieter on Three because one of its occupants was dead or unconscious. Now, he could hear heavy breathing and the thud of blows being struck. Reminding himself that it was virtually impossible to land heavy blows in the weightless condition did no good, because he was remembering the girl's long, dark hair and imagining one fist gripping a handful of it while the other pounded her into insensibility. . . .

"Pod Ten. Retro thrust completed and I can see two other pods. I think one of them is close enough to wave to."

"Save your energy," said Mercer dully.

The sounds from Three were taking on a new quality because the purpose of the man making them had also changed. His world might only have minutes of life left to it, and he, whichever of the two it was, intended enjoying them to the full—the gasping, chopped-up monologue made that all too plain. But his intentions, which would easily have been accomplished on Earth, where gravity kept inanimate or unconscious objects in one place, in his present environment required the active cooperation of both parties. But one of the parties was unconscious and could not have cooperated even if she had wanted to, and he was becoming angrier, hotter and more frustrated by the second.

Suddenly his breathing became stertorous. The sounds of cursing and the slapping contact of his body against the plastic stopped. He began to make choking noises, and a few seconds later he was making no sound at all.

Mercer swore horribly and turned up the volume on the pod frequency. The segment was suddenly filled with the sounds of heavy, labored, gasping breathing. It was coming from the fourteen other survival capsules and not, he was afraid, from Pod Three.

"Prescott. I heard that, Mercer. You might be better advised to divert to Pod Four. The Corries could be shorter of air than they realize. MacArdle will give you the figures. Neilson will meet you and come aboard at Four—we'll need to make some fast pickups by then, and for that we need fast and fancy maneuvering."

"I have to check Three."

"I see. In that case, MacArdle wants you to observe your target pod carefully so as to note the rate of apparent drift in the stars beyond it. This will tell him how much you are off course and allow him to compute an angle of thrust which will compensate for it during deceleration. Neilson will give you a rundown on the automatic docking sequence."

"I'm listening," said Mercer.

"When they've finished, you should check on the Captain's condition, if you haven't already done so. You are going to be very busy for the next ten hours."

"Will do."

But all at once Mercer did not want to check on Three's drift, nor did he want to see proof of the things he had heard going on, even though the sight might not be as bad as his imagination had pictured it. Pod Three was in all probability a coffin which would never be opened—it might drift in space for all eternity, beyond even the range of Gabriel's trumpet, unless he himself went in and disordered the bones of its freshly dead.

There was no real need for him to open that stinking, plastic coffin. The air must have been used up during that long, vicious fight, and a man who had killed once by strangling his victim might lack the imagination during a stress situation to vary his methods of coercion. Mrs. Mathewson could well have been dead before her attacker had succumbed to the heat and asphyxiation himself.

Mercer was no stranger to the sight of death, whether naturally occurring or violent, but he was most desperately anxious not to see Mrs. Mathewson dead. For the first time, he was able to understand why some people refused to look at the bodies of even their nearest and dearest relatives. If one remembered them only as they were when they were alive, then they still lived after a fashion, because there was no real proof that their life had ended.

He could still call Prescott and change his mind. But then there was the boy to think about. Young Mathewson might not be as good at playing spaceman as he sounded. He might be headed wide of the rendezvous point and already condemned to die. But he might not die; Mercer might have to tell him that his mother had died, and he realized that, no matter how bad it was going to make him feel a few hours from now, he had to be able to tell the boy that she had died before he reached her pod.

While MacArdle gave him instructions, he checked on the Captain's condition and made sure that the services in the other bunks were functioning. Then Neilson's voice filled the segment, interrupted only by passengers saying that they could see other pods, that their air was running out, that it was very hot, and When would the recovery ship arrive? People, Prescott included, were not giving Mercer much time to think, for which he was glad.

As his segment was closing with Three he wondered what he would do if there was a survivor in the pod who was not the girl. He knew what he wanted to do, but a rebel bunch of brain cells in his mind—a minority group, but one which was steadily gaining converts—kept insisting that in different circumstances Three's occupants might well have become good friends, that the twin disasters of *Eurydice* blowing up and one of the three being female had subjected two flawed personalities to the breaking strain—and that the innocent one, who had given no indication of being flawed, had perished as well.

But the minority group would not accept that, and insisted on being stupidly optimistic.

With MacArdle's help he found himself less than twenty yards from Pod Three and drifting very slowly past it. Mercer had an air bottle and mask strapped in position, another set drifting loosely at his elbow, and the inside seal of the airlock already open. Through the window in the outer seal he could see Three turning slowly end over end like a great fat cucumber which was half silvered and half clear. In the transparent section he could see a motionless tangle of plastic screens, clothing, food containers, and bodies floating like strange fish in a pink-tinged, frozen ocean.

When Three's lock turned to face his position, he launched the automatic docking cable; he watched its seeking head home onto the lock transmitter, connect, and begin drawing the two vehicles together. As the cable shortened, their difference in velocity set them spinning about their common center of gravity. By the time the lock interfaces came together they were spinning quite fast—not enough to blur the stars, but enough for Mercer to feel the tugging of artificial gravity.

He checked that the passenger frequency was switched off and reported to Prescott what was happening. Then he opened the connecting seals and went through.

The centrifugal force was greater than he had expected, so that he dropped not too lightly onto the services panel at the opposite end of the pod. It was covered with a sexless tangle of arms and legs and plastic debris, and the whole mess was splattered with the sticky red discs of congealed blood which, a few minutes earlier, had been drifting weightless in the incredibly hot and stinking air. The smell was forcing its way past his breathing mask, so that he had to fight to keep from retching.

Mercer began pulling the tangle apart, trying to separate and identify the people. The Sun whirled steadily around them, plunging them into darkness for a few seconds, then sending shadows crawling over the bodies, which gave them a semblance of movement and life.

Two of the bodies, both male, were covered by thick traceries of nail marks. It was as if they were wearing red-embroidered body stockings whose patterns included a large number of solid red flowers—the places where they had used their teeth on each other. Wet red patches showed on their scalps where hair had been pulled out, their ears were like raw meat, and he doubted if one of them had been able to see at the end. Neither of the two men was sweating, nor did they bleed.

Mrs. Mathewson was also bloody, but it did not seem to be her own. She was at the bottom of the heap, her head under a piece of plastic screen, which also covered the air supply outlet in what would have been an effective oxygen tent if the air being vented had been more than fractionally less foul than that in the pod itself. There were two large bumps on the right side of her skull, no depressions, and the side of her face and upper torso showed severe bruising. She did not appear to be breathing, but her pulse was weak and very rapid.

Mercer slipped the spare mask over her head and

turned the air tap on full. He tried to inflate her lungs by moving her arms rhythmically away and back to her sides, but he had to be careful because she was so emaciated that he could actually see two cracked ribs. The pulse began to slow and strengthen, although she showed no sign of regaining consciousness.

He was dizzy from a combination of the stench, the heat, and sheer relief. Quickly and carefully he strapped on her air-tank, checked the mask fastenings, and lifted her in his arms. He bent at the knees and then jumped for the lock seal eight feet above his head.

The services panel gave under his feet; his center of gravity was not lined up properly with his center of thrust, and they began a slow somersault. Although the centrifugal force was weak, it was still strong enough to bring them to a stop three feet short of the seal, and they began to fall slowly back. When they landed, the pod stretched alarmingly, its walls closed in, and for an awful moment Mercer thought that the plastic would rupture and burst. But slowly the capsule resumed its proper shape, and Mercer tried again.

This time he did not jump immediately. Instead, he made a series of knee flexions, which set the pod bouncing slowly in and out and its walls pulsing like some alien artificial heart. He could hardly see, with the sweat pouring into his eyes, and he knew that if he gave in to the urge to be sick he would gum up his breathing mask and probably suffocate or collapse from heat prostration before he could get it cleared. So he persisted, reinforcing the up and down movement of the services panel until regular contractions threatened to bounce him away; then he jumped during one particularly strong upswing.

"The girl is all right," he reported when they were back in his segment. He hardly recognized his own voice.

"Good. I didn't really think that the air would last."

"It lasted," said Mercer, "because the other two had stopped using it."

"In that case, leave them and mark the pod. Seal up and prepare to break contact. But before you do, Mac-Ardle says he can utilize your present spin to boost you towards Neilson and Pod Four. It could save a lot of time, and the Corries have very little time left. I am closing with Pod Five now and will be too busy to talk to you for a while, so I'll give you MacArdle—"

"Before you open the seal," said Mercer, "take two anti-nausea tablets and plug your nostrils with cotton."

"I'm supposed to be giving the orders."

"Doctor's orders," said Mercer firmly, "you have to take."

Chapter XX

On the way to the rendezvous with Neilson and Pod Four, Mercer had time to move Mrs. Mathewson into the bunk below the Captain's and carry out a proper examination and tape her broken ribs. She still had not regained consciousness, but the reason, he was sure, was nothing more serious than a bad concussion. While he worked, the last few pods were nearing the rendezvous area, and his speaker kept repeating the occupants' complaints about the heat and shortage of air. Some of the passengers sounded close to desperation.

After his few minutes in Pod Three, Mercer wondered why they were not raving mad.

Then suddenly it was the slow, deliberate voice of Neilson, relayed through Prescott's transmitter, that was filling his segment.

"I'll be docking with you in a few minutes, Mercer, but don't open your seal until I tell you. The drill is that I push you close to Four, disengage, then let you reel them in as you did with Three. I'll position you so that you will not have to worry about spin. When you have them aboard, dump the pod; then I'll redock and join you. Got that?"

"It sounds almost too easy," said Mercer.

After one unpleasant surprise when he opened the seal—his ears popped painfully because Four's pressurization was dangerously low—it all went surprisingly easily. There was no centrifugal force to complicate the rescue, the pod interior was uncluttered, and both of the

163

Corries were just barely conscious. It took only a few minutes to float them inside, toss in a marker grenade with a five-minute delay, seal up, and detach from the pod.

Neilson's segment moved in quickly, nudged the empty pod aside, and locked on.

Mercer turned to see Mrs. Corrie taking off her breathing mask, while her husband stared through the canopy at the slowly shrinking shape of their capsule. Corrie gave a startled grunt when the transparent section of the pod abruptly changed to a dazzling white.

"A small explosive charge inside a bulb of white paint," Mercer explained. "It marks the empty pods so that we will know to leave them alone. But you two will be much more comfortable in bunks—"

"No," said Mrs Corrie, gripping her husband's arm with both hands.

"Excuse me," said Mercer, giving them each a hefty shot of sedative. As their eyes began to lose focus, he went on: "There is nothing to be afraid of, m'am, not now. The bunks are designed for seriously ill or injured passengers and carry their own life-support and waste elimination equipment. They are cool and roomy—"

"How roomy?" asked Corrie.

"If you are worrying about feeling claustrophobia, don't. You will be asleep and . . ."

Neilson arrived at that point, just as Mercer had decided that he knew what was really worrying Mrs. Corrie. The engineer was wearing a shiny patina of sweat and had his cap pulled well down over his eyes. Mercer wondered if Neilson had a bald patch and was self-conscious about it; then he realized that it was a means of protecting the engineer's eyes while checking marker stars close to the Sun.

He turned back to the Corries.

"I expect you don't want to be separated after all that you've been through," he said. "That is quite all right—the bunks are big enough to fit two in a pinch. But I'll have to increase the air supply accordingly. . . ."

Neilson made the necessary adjustments and helped Mercer fit the already sleeping couple into their bunk.

"I don't approve of single beds, either," said the engineer.

"Head to toe like that, there isn't much risk of them suffocating unless someone puts a foot in the other's mouth," said Mercer worriedly. "But I think I'll leave the sides open and keep an eye on them anyway. It's nice to see you, Neilson."

"Likewise, Mercer."

"Prescott. Delay your reunion celebrations, please. MacArdle has some figures for you. . . ."

A few minutes later, Neilson had instructions for Mercer.

"We have to reach Pods One and Nine as quickly as possible," said the engineer, removing the cover of Mercer's thrust panel as he spoke, "and pushing you ahead of me will waste too much time. So I want you to apply thrust to your segment while I do the same with mine—that way we will approach the targets broadside on but much faster. Ignore all the pretty lights unless they suddenly turn red. Depress this stud when I tell you—I'll give you a five-second countdown—and release it when I yell 'Cut.'

"The procedure is the same when we close with the pods, which are only a short distance apart," he added. "But first I have to get us properly lined up."

"Two pods in trouble," said Mercer, reaching for the switch of the passenger transmitter. "That's six people —no, seven, because Ten has four aboard—and we do not have an unlimited number of empty bunks."

"Don't touch it, Mercer," said Neilson sharply. "Prescott has been monitoring that frequency while you were busy, and I don't want anything to distract you until we're on our way. And anyhow, you have established a useful precedent with the Corries. . . ."

The passengers in Pods One and Nine were in no condition to object to being packed in two to a bunk— they were much too relieved at being able to breathe relatively cool air again, and for the few minutes which it took for the sedative shots to take effect, Mercer let then assume that such overcrowding was normal.

While he was dealing with them he could not help noticing the bunk temperature gauges, which showed the differential between the segment as a whole and that being experienced by his patients. The new arrivals were generating a lot of extra heat, and Mercer could feel as well as see the difference.

Before the engineer could rejoin Mercer, Prescott was telling them that MacArdle had more figures for them. Pod Six was running out of air now. Neilson estimated that they would need twenty minutes to reach them.

When they were on their way, Mercer asked about Pod Eight, which had accelerated past the rendezvous and been chased by MacArdle. He had been out of touch and nobody had mentioned them recently.

"That was quite a chase, Mercer. It will take me five hours to get back there, but I have them aboard."

"Are they all right?"

"Two of them are doing fine. But the other man, Saddler, is running a bluff with a pair of threes."

"Prescott. When you've dealt with Six, there are two other pods, Ten and Thirteen, who will be in bad trouble by then. Give Neilson their markers, MacArdle, or would you rather watch the poker game?"

"How," whispered Mercer, "does he know which pods are in trouble?"

"He noted their positions as they came in," said Neilson quietly, "and his telescope brings in the pods that went wide. From his position they have a wide angle of separation, so he lines up his directional antenna on the telescope bearing. This increases the strength of any given pod's signal and so he knows who is calling for help even if they don't identify themselves, or even if they are so short of air that they can't speak."

"Do we have a dish antenna?" Mercer asked. "I was thinking that it might operate in reverse to allow me to speak to a pod without all the other pods hearing the message."

Neilson shook his head. "Only the Captain's segment has such refinements, and normally the dish is used to maintain two-way contact with *Eurydice* Control. But now Prescott is using it on the pod frequency, because if Control and MacArdle haven't done their calculations right, there isn't much point in wasting time talking to Earth with passengers in trouble only a few miles away. . . ."

"Suppose MacArdle or Control haven't—" began Mercer.

". . . This segment, on the other hand," Neilson went on firmly, "has no sophisticated communications equipment, a relatively small fuel reserve, and quite a lot of power and air reserves—a life raft, Mercer, is what we're in."

"If I'd known that," said Mercer, "I might have wasted a little of the power keeping the place cooler. But about the recovery ship—"

"You will be very glad that you didn't," said Neilson very seriously. "This segment takes thirteen passengers and a crew of two, comfortably. So far you've squeezed in ten passengers and have saved on space because most of them have doubled up. Trouble is, you can't double the air supply. Our segments have less elbow room and can take three survivors in a pinch, and how Prescott is managing with four I shudder to think.

"Why don't you take a few minutes to visit my place?" he added. "It's through the airlock and then straight ahead. You can't miss it."

"Are you trying to be funny, Neilson?" Mercer said harshly. "Trying to humor me, perhaps, so that I won't ask awkward questions? Do you *know* when the recovery ship is due?"

"If I did know I might not tell you. You would only worry if it was a little late."

"I'm not completely stupid. If it doesn't arrive exactly on time, that means it has gone wide and won't arrive at all. That is so, isn't it?"

Neilson did not reply. Instead he cocked his head to one side and said, "One of your patients wants out."

The Captain was tapping the inside of his bunk and growing audibly more impatient with every passing second. Mercer started to say that Collingwood had no business being awake at all, then stopped because he realized that he must have missed giving the Captain his last sedative shot. He moved quickly to the bunk, opened the side, and slid the litter far enough out to see what his patient was doing. He had another shot ready, but it would take a few minutes for it to take effect, and longer if Collingwood was trying to resist it.

He hoped the Captain would not start to act up— not now, with Neilson here, most of the other bunks filled with lightly sleeping passengers, and less than fifteen minutes to go before they picked up another batch of survivors.

Collingwood had stopped tapping and was using his fingers to explore the bandages covering his eyes. He winced as the needle slid in, then said sharply, "Who is that?"

"Mercer, sir."

Neilson drifted up and gave a little sigh of sympathy as he saw the bandages, the lead shielding on Collingwood's chest and side, and the livid decompression blotches covering the Captain's body. He withdrew again without speaking.

"I've lost count of the times that I have begun to come to," said the Captain, "and you've jabbed me to sleep again. I want out of this thing, Mercer—even if I can't see, I can still hear, speak and think, dammit. And I should be getting exercise to prevent muscle atrophy and other . . . But you're the doctor and should know all about that."

"Yes, sir," said Mercer. "That was done while you were out—gentle exercise and massage every four hours. But I strongly advise you to stay put, sir. Movement of any kind could aggravate your present condition—"

"Which is?"

The shot was showing no sign of taking effect and, Mercer knew, the Captain was demanding nothing more or less than a condition report on the hunk of sophisticated organic machinery that was his body, and it was very obvious that he did not want the report colored by medical double-talk. Through the canopy behind Neilson he could see their next pod growing slowly larger, so he told the Captain about his condition and the various reasons why he should not move or risk exposing his damaged eyes to the light. He kept it brief and to the point, and completely accurate.

"But you must have changed the dressings while I was sleeping," Collingwood said when he had finished. "And presumably the damage caused by dim light is no greater when I am awake than asleep. I want to know if I can see, Doctor. And while you are taking off the dressings you can tell me about the condition of your segment, the other crew segments and the pods. . . ."

He had other questions as well, and there was still no sign of the sedative taking effect.

Mercer looked appealingly at Neilson, who moved closer and began answering the more technical questions as the last few layers were being removed. Mercer was relieved to discover that his segment was in good shape, pleased that Neilson thought him something less than wasteful of its power reserves, and surprised at the multiplicity of activities of the other officers during times when Mercer had thought he was the only one doing any work—reassuring the passengers had been a very small job compared to that of organizing their rescue.

When the bandages and pads were off, Collingwood kept his eyes closed while Neilson went on speaking.

Perhaps he is asleep at last, Mercer thought, or maybe he's just afraid to look in case there is nothing to see.

"If opening your eyes feels as if it might hurt them," Mercer said, "don't do it. We're turned away from the Sun, and the only light is coming from a pod about half a mile away, so it may be too dim for anything at all to register. . . ."

Collingwood opened his eyes then. In the dim light the whites looked almost as dark as the irises—they were still very bloodshot—and smeared with cream. Mercer saw them twitch from side to side, then up and down, then the Captain sighed and closed them.

"I can't stay awake any longer," he said, "and Prescott is doing all the right things. But a word of advice, Mercer. Before you meet him again, shave, and for god's sake put on some clothes. . . ."

Neilson's sigh of relief warmed the back of his neck as Mercer began replacing the dressings, and the mental picture that he had been seeing of an ex-Captain Collingwood, blind and with a lung burned out and probably cancerous, being led around by his beautiful young wife until she became his prematurely aged widow, faded away. Suddenly he laughed and said, "He can *see*."

"Yes," said Neilson, "but we're due to decelerate in three minutes. You know the drill."

At first Mercer was sure that Prescott had directed them to the wrong pod, one that was already marked as being empty. But when he opened the seal he discovered that the life-support system must have packed up only a few minutes earlier, and that the pod interior was filled with a dense, stinking fog. He had to grope through the weightless welter of plastic screens, clothing and other drifting debris for something which felt like part of a human being. He found two of them near the services panel and pushed them gently towards the seal at the opposite side of the capsule.

The third survivor found him, wrapping his or her arms tightly around his neck from the back like someone who was drowning. The breathing mask was knocked away from his face and suddenly Mercer was drowning, too, in air which had to be too foul to support life. He lost his bearings as well, and could not even guess where the seal was. He kicked hard against anything solid or near solid with which he came in contact, sending the passenger and himself bouncing blindly between the plastic walls of the pod. By sheer luck he found himself tumbling into his segment, which was by then also filled with stinking fog.

A few minutes later, while the active survivor was helping him resuscitate his two companions, Neilson put his head and shoulders in to say, "Prescott has another one for us. We're already lined up. Seven seconds thrust, five seconds countdown. Your mouth is bleeding, Mercer."

While Neilson and Mercer emptied three more pods, the Mathewson boy in Fourteen was given his marker stars and thrust timing, with Fifteen and Sixteen timed to arrive a few minutes later. When they came aboard, the last batch of passengers said that Mercer's segment smelled worse than the pod they had just left, that it was much hotter as well, and had he anything to eat? Mercer told them that talking wasted air, and he tried to find a place for them where they would not be in the way during the next rescue operation—the last rescue operation, Mercer was sure, because his segment and its services were becoming dangerously overloaded.

Neilson had locked his control panel against accidental activation and placed three passengers in his segment. Two more drifted between the connecting seals, their feet in the engineer's vehicle and their heads in Mercer's segment. The bunks now held eighteen, and the spaces between, another two, excluding Neilson and Mercer, who were pressed against a canopy that was virtually opaque with condensation.

From time to time they rubbed it with sweating hands to search the blurred stars for the recovery ship. Despite everything that Mercer told them about conserving energy and air, the passengers were beginning to argue and push and ask why two of the bunk sides were still up when all the others were down and contributing their quota of air to the rest of the passengers. The occupants of the bunks, whose original sedative shots were beginning to wear off, had begun to complain about being hot and cramped and unable to breathe, while the people outside were angrily offering to change places with them.

"Those two bunks contain patients, as opposed to mere survivors," said Mercer sharply. "Neither of them is pleasant to look at, and one of them, the Captain, is slightly radioactive. . . ."

He went on to describe the Captain's injuries in detail, the recovery of his sight, and his poor chance of survival if some method of removing the two specks of radioactive material in his lung was not discovered within the next few weeks. Medical facilities on board the recovery ship would be no better than those on *Eurydice,* and if Collingwood was not treated soon, although he would still be alive at the end of the voyage, it would only be for a couple of years after that.

As he continued talking, Mercer knew that he had their undivided attention, and he realized once again why morale was always good in a hospital ward—suffering shared was suffering halved, and there was always somebody there in poorer shape than oneself. He was also doing his best to take their minds forward to the time when they would be in the recovery ship, and past the time in the not-too-distant future when the ship might or might not arrive. He could see them thinking about the Captain's misfortunes instead of their own, and a few of them were putting forward suggestions for treatment when there was an interruption.

The First Officer was trying to give them something else to think about as well.

"*Prescott. Switch on your pod frequency, Mercer.*"

Mercer pushed between two passengers to do so, and heard the Mathewson boy's voice.

". . . *Didn't answer last time because Mr. Prescott said you were busy with passengers, but you can talk to me now. Pod Fourteen retro burn complete, and I can see two other pods . . .*"

"Prescott. We have him."

". . . *and one of them is all white. What do I do now, Mercer?*"

"Nice shooting, Mathewson," said Mercer warmly. "We have you in sight. Your orders? Well, keep a sharp lookout for the recovery ship, but don't look at or near the Sun without goggles. Acknowledge, please."

"*Pod Fourteen. Will do.*"

But the concern of the passengers for the Captain and their relief at the Mathewson boy's safe arrival in the rendezvous area were short-lived emotions, and soon they were saying that the boy was lucky to have a pod's air and food supply all to himself, that the recovery ship was not coming, that it would be impossible to see it if it did come with the canopy fogged with condensation, that it was hot, and that if some unprintable didn't keep his feet out of someone else's mouth he would get them bitten off.

"You must understand," said Mercer, trying not to gasp between words as everyone else was doing, "that we and the other pods and segments are following our original course for Ganymede and will arrive exactly on time. The recovery ship is virtually identical to *Eurydice* except for the extra boosters, which enable it to catch up with us and decelerate to match our velocity, and which also make it impossible for it to be manned, because no human being could survive the enormous acceleration. These boosters are very powerful, and if they are fired in the rendezvous area we, or some of us at least, might suffer even more from the heat. So the recovery ship has got to feel its way in, guided by the First Officer, and the time of arrival is dictated by considerations of survivor safety. It could be only minutes away, or a couple of hours. Isn't that so, Neilson?"

The engineer rubbed at the canopy condensation with one hand. Three fingers were outspread with the thumb bent inwards, indicating three, possibly three-and-a-half hours. Aloud, he said, "That is an oversimplification, Mercer, but essentially correct."

His expression, which only Mercer could see, was saying *Lies, all lies.*

Three or more hours, Mercer thought. He went on, "And we have ample air and power to last out?"

"Yes, of course," said Neilson, but his expression had not changed.

Nobody spoke for a few minutes, but Mercer knew that they would speak soon. Then they would start pushing and cursing and fighting, for no other reasons than that it was hot and stuffy and that these were the worst things they could do.

Mercer wiped sweat from his forearm and saw fresh globules grow a few seconds later. He had never been a compulsive extrovert, never enjoyed the shouting, sweating proximity of his fellow men even when it had been necessary on various occasions. He knew, with an awful certainty, that he could not take much more of this and that he would probably be the one who started the chain-reaction of violence, for the simple reason that he had either to get out of it or end it.

The heat and humidity was worse than it had been in many of the pods he had entered. He could understand how Kirk and Stone had felt, although their original reason for fighting had been much stronger, if not better, than his. Either he had to get out, or he wanted all the other quarreling, stinking people to get out.

He suddenly realized that he could put them out, although not literally. . . .

"Mr. Neilson and I will have to sweat it out," Mercer said, forcing a laugh so that they would all know he was making a joke, "but there is no necessity for the rest of you to share our discomfort. What I am proposing isn't in accordance with company regulations, of course, which state that medical stores should be used only on passengers who are ill or injured. Apart from being hungry and a little short of breath, there is nothing wrong with you people, but you would be still more comfortable if—"

"If the air is so scarce," said a man beside him in a voice close to being hysterical, "why the hell are you talking so much?"

Mercer closed his eyes for a moment, fighting a sudden and incredibly violent urge to batter the hateful, unshaven face and hunger-and-heat-emaciated body until it looked like the two he had left in Pod Three. But he knew that once he started he would not be able to stop with this one stupid, sarcastic passenger—he would go berserk among them all, until they were all quiet and probably all dead. He wondered why he was having these intensely violent thoughts; then he felt the heat and stench and the sweaty pressure of bodies all around him and decided that he was in hell and that in hell everybody acted like the Devil.

"If I talk, everyone else listens, sir," he said, opening his eyes, "and that saves more air than if everyone talks. What I intend to do is give some of you the opportunity of taking special shots—a form of mild sedative, really, which also opens the pores and makes it feel cooler even if it isn't. I will use a spray injection hypo, which is quite painless, and if you'll give me just a moment I'll demonstrate. . . ."

It wasn't all lies, Mercer told himself cynically. The shots were painless, but the recipients would feel cooler and more comfortable because they would be out cold for the next three hours. And if he pretended that there were not enough shots to go around, that he was doing most of them a favor, they might not resist the idea until it was too late. Certainly the first three did not resist, possibly because he had led them to believe that he was still demonstrating the painlessness of the procedure and nothing else. Still talking reassuringly, he injected any arm or thigh that presented itself.

He looked at Neilson, who nodded and wriggled

alongside him and began moving the suddenly relaxed bodies out of the way, holding the ones who argued or tried to break free, and closing bunks so that Mercer could reach the passengers in the lower tiers. Only one passenger, the last one of the three packed into Neilson's segment, put up any resistance. She said, "We're not going to wake up again, are we?"

"No, m'am," said Mercer, "at least, not in here." Silently he added, *We hope.*

A few minutes later, Neilson gently cleared the space above his panel of drifting bodies and said, "Putting them out was a good idea, Mercer. I've rechecked my calculations, and provided we don't waste air in needless discussion, we might just make it."

"Fine," said Mercer.

"I'm not trying to tell you your job, Mercer," he went on, "but you might have to use a little energy checking that these sleeping beauties don't drift too close to each other and smother. Or have you got that under control?"

"Yes."

"It's hot."

"Yes."

"About the Captain, Mercer. I should have told you earlier, but the passengers were so interested in his troubles that I didn't want to spoil things for them. We reported what you said about his condition before *Eurydice* blew, and the recovery ship will be carrying the special instruments you need to operate on him and withdraw the radioactive materials."

"That's great."

"Prescott will be acting Captain for the rest of the trip out and back—Collingwood won't be able to assume command again until he has passed the Earthside medical. Prescott should have been Captain anyway, but the company thought he lacked charm for a passenger ship skipper and put Collingwood in with Prescott to keep him right. The Captain was strictly a station shuttle man—a nice person, but it wasn't fair on

Prescott. He is tops in this profession, but he needs something—"

"A good PR man?"

"Yeah. But we shouldn't waste air talking all the time."

"You are doing most of it."

"Listen, Mercer, are you asking for a punch in the —"

"Prescott. The remaining pods seem to be in no immediate danger, with the exception of one. There is a life-support system failure with toxic wastes escaping into the living space. This is an urgent one, Mercer. Can you squeeze in three more?"

The three survivors were sedated just as soon as Mercer was sure that they were still alive. Then he burrowed and pushed until he found spaces for them, and returned to the canopy to rest for the effort of burrowing in again a few minutes later to make sure that nobody was smothering. That effort increased the heat being generated inside the segment, and the precaution did not seem to be really necessary. Twice he nearly passed out, and once he almost panicked. Only the thought of Kirk as he had last seen him saved Mercer from tearing and kicking at the bodies that were pressing in all around him.

In a way, Kirk's reaction had been normal. He had known that he was going to die and had decided to enjoy himself first. But the hot, intimate contact of flesh did not stir Mercer, even though, like Kirk, he was sure that he was going to die shortly. He began to wonder why, and if there was anything wrong with him. But then he began to realize that all there was wrong with him was a recently contracted and serious case of monogamy, because the only close contact he wanted or would enjoy would be with the patient in bunk Three.

He did not go among the passengers again, but stayed close to the canopy, fighting for every breath and sweating from every pore. This atmosphere is unsuited to human life, he told himself, so why don't we all die?

But they did not die, and some of the passengers seemed to be moving, waking up—but it was only Neilson pushing his way through to the canopy.

"I thought it might be cooler here," he said. "It isn't."

Mercer wiped at the plastic without speaking.

"I feel like a living fish in a can of sardines," said Neilson, then added, "Sorry, I'm talking."

The silence stretched for a sweating, stifling eternity, and when it was broken, the voice was not using their precious air.

"Pod Fourteen; Mathewson. Come in, Mercer."

The voice was without expression, just like that of a real spaceman in an emergency. Mercer wondered what had gone wrong in Fourteen and if he could squeeze in one more. It would have to be a bad emergency for the medical segment to be a sanctuary, but it was only right that a mother and son should be together at the end.

"Mercer," he said.

"I . . . I have visual contact with the recovery ship, Mercer."

"Prescott. Confirmed. MacArdle will have the figures for you in—"

They lost Prescott for a few minutes then because the Mathewson boy had lost control and was whooping like an Indian, and Neilson and Mercer were joining him.

Chapter XXI

The recovery ship differed from *Eurydice* in that it had two passenger locks aft instead of one, a feature designed to speed the re-embarkation of survivors. Neilson nudged Mercer's segment against one and used the other to dock his own vehicle; but it was a very close thing, because Mercer's head was pounding and throbbing, and black splotches were blotting out his vision when he hit the quick-release on his seal. Then the hot, putrid air was rushing past him and cool, dry air began seeping back. He crawled out, shivering, to find Neilson already waiting for him.

"We'll have to go after the others as soon as possible," said the engineer briskly. "Do you mind if I don't help you unload this bunch? If I can concentrate on replenishing your segment with power cells, air tanks, and fuel cartridges, we could be ready to go in thirty minutes."

Mercer nodded. He began moving out the sleeping passengers and floating them carefully into the main compartment, which now seemed to be enormous. He began with the people in Neilson's segment, because it had to be jettisoned to allow Prescott, who was estimating contact with the recovery ship in twenty minutes, to dock. MacArdle and his passengers were due half an hour later, by which time Prescott's segment would have been turned loose. Mercer's vehicle was the one designed for fast rescue work, so long as there was at least one trained astronaut aboard to fly it.

The last two people he moved out were the Captain and Mrs. Mathewson, and these he took up to sick bay. The place gave him the strangest feeling of disorientation because it was exactly the same as the place he had just left, except for its fresh, newly-minted look. On his way he saw that the people drifting about the passenger compartment were showing signs of animation. He checked his dive, letting Mrs. Mathewson and the Captain fall slowly ahead of him, while he spoke to them.

The manual had told him what to say. He had read that particular section over and over again during the past two weeks, like a fairy story which he had never expected to come true.

"Your attention, ladies and gentlemen," he said. "As you can see, your couches are already arranged in cruising mode and numbered as were the positions in *Eurydice*. In the usual compartments you will find food and fresh clothing. Will you please go to your original couches, strap in, talk as much as you want to, but keep the center of this compartment clear. For the next few hours the ship's officers will be bringing in the remaining survivors and doing other necessary jobs, and you may feel that you are being ignored, but things will soon return to normal.

"By the day after tomorrow," he added, smiling, "I may even be able to arrange a swim in the tank."

When he had completed his check on the Captain, he replaced the blankets removed during the superheated period in the other segment and immobilized Collingwood with webbing. The bunks were not cold, but the feel of blankets would give a sense of security, and Mrs. Mathewson certainly needed that. But she came to just as he was about to slide back her bunk, and she began to struggle against the webbing and blanket with increasing violence. Instinctively he put out his hands to restrain her, then he remembered the position and severity of some of her bruises and reached for the hypo instead.

"Take it easy, m'am," he said gently. "You're safe now."

She stopped struggling and said, "Mercer?"

"Yes, m'am."

He knew that he should sedate her quickly before she had a chance to think, to remember. But she could not go through the rest of her life under sedation, and it was important that she should try to face those ugly memories as soon as possible—not completely, of course, but in easy stages. He desperately wanted to see her reactions, to get some idea whether or not she would be able to handle it, before he used the hypo. Neilson hadn't called him, so there was still a little time before he had to leave.

"Bobby?"

"He's safe, too, but still in his pod. You must understand that having it to himself means that he won't run out of air as quickly as the others. We have to bring him in last, m'am."

"I know. You could give him no preferential treatment. You acted as if he was a man."

"He did a man's job, m'am, and when he cried like a frightened little boy for his mother, I pretended not to hear."

"And you brought him back. I'm grateful. I might not sound it, but I am. You treated him exactly right, said all the proper things—to all of us, not just to Bobby. You were always cool, calm and . . . and nothing seemed to touch you or change you in any way. I suppose I should be glad, we should all be glad, that you weren't an over-sympathetic character. . . ."

As she fell silent, Mercer thought that clinically he was very pleased with her reactions, but that on the personal level he was coming off very badly. He wished he could relax and stop saying 'm'am' and radiating the composure which he most decidedly did not feel.

"I'm not supposed to display signs of weakness in front of the passengers," Mercer said irritably, "and especially not before my patients, but if you knew me better you would realize that I could be quite bad-tempered at times, and jealous, and very, very angry in certain circumstances—"

"I'm sorry, Doctor," she broke in. "I don't know why I'm picking on you like this." She put her hand out of the blanket and gripped his, the one which wasn't holding the hypo, and went on: "Don't put me out again just yet. I'm picking on you because I can't get nasty with myself—at least, not out loud. When you were talking to us back there I could tell that you were angry sometimes, and that you couldn't afford to show it because everybody else was listening and would have known what was going on in Three. But you knew, and you made Kirk and Stone mad at you because you were like an over-amplified voice of conscience. You kept heading them off, talking sense, lecturing them. If it hadn't been for you, it would have happened much sooner. Are they both . . . both . . .?"

Her grip was so tight that his fingers were turning white. He nodded.

"Maybe I should not have been so hard to get," she went on, but pleading with him with her eyes to argue and disagree with everything she was saying. "These days nobody would have worried, would they? And you would not have talked about it. But they were strangers, just like my husband was several different kinds of stranger before he died, and all the different strangers wanted to make love to me. And it was so open out there, so clean and bright and empty, so I couldn't—it would have been like sinning in Heaven.

"But I could have forced myself, and once I almost did," she said, looking away from him. "If they'd had me, they might not have started fighting."

Mercer shook his head. "Then I would have had to lecture you, at very inconvenient times, about the need to avoid generating heat."

Still she would not look at him as she said, "After he knocked me out, what happened?"

"Nothing much," said Mercer. "He became angry

and frustrated, very angry and extremely frustrated from what I could hear—and I was listening very carefully, you understand. Then he collapsed and died from heat-stroke a few minutes later, leaving just enough air to keep you alive until I arrived. But you should try to forget all about it, you know. It's over. And you've a grip like a wrestler, m'am. If I'm to perform any more miracles of surgery you'd better not break my fingers."

"You aren't telling the truth," she said angrily, still without letting go. "You know it is important to me, and you just want me to think—"

"It's important to me, too," Mercer broke in quietly. "Not vitally important, you understand, but still important enough to make me glad that I'm not lying."

"I'm not sure that I understand you," she said, but her expression said that she did, and her grip on his hand eased. She added, "Will I have to tell people about it? Will there be an investigation?"

"Not unless you want to," said Mercer. "So far as I'm concerned, I don't really know who did what to whom. Both men were unrecognizable when I got to them, and once I knew that they were dead and you weren't, I couldn't waste time reconstructing the crime. If you like, I can say, quite truthfully, that one died from asphyxiation and one from heat-stroke. That isn't the whole truth, of course, but I'm thinking about Mrs. Kirk's feelings as well as yours and Bobby's, and even you don't know for sure what happened at the end. Nobody has jurisdiction in spacewreck incidents like this, so there is no point in talking about it if you don't want to. The only people who would be interested are the news media, and they—"

"No," she said firmly.

"I didn't think you would want that," he said, bringing up the hypo. "So just try to forget the whole thing for the time being, and sleep. And let go of my hand. You'll be in this bunk until your cracked ribs mend, so you can expect to see a lot more of me. . . ."

He stopped. She was laughing, and wincing, because it must have been hurting her ribs.

"Is that possible?" she said.

Mercer smiled in return. "I can't answer that, m'am, until you are completely recovered. There are rules about doctor-patient relationships, you know."

Before she could reply he had tucked her bare arm under the blanket and closed the bunk.

She had made him aware for the first time in two weeks that he was improperly dressed, that he was not even wearing a cap, as Neilson was, and that they were no longer in an emergency situation in which such lapses could be excused. He still had a few minutes to spare before the engineer needed him, so he shaved, climbed into a set of clean uniform coveralls, and used the canopy plastic to check that his cap was straight. The sooner everything returned to normal the better, he thought as he turned to go.

"Neilson. I will need you in ten minutes, Mercer— this took a little longer than expected. Prescott is back on board and wants to see you in the control-room."

"Mercer. Ten minutes."

The First Officer was in Neilson's position, going over the engineering tell-tales. He looked at Mercer slowly from head to toes and shook his head.

He said, "Before you leave to pick up the rest of the survivors, I want you to remember that there will be an inquiry when we get back to Earth into the *Eurydice* disaster and the proper functioning or otherwise of its survival equipment. Neilson, MacArdle and myself will be responsible for the technical evidence, and you will deal with questions regarding the effects on passengers. You will also have to give medical evidence regarding the deaths of Kirk and Stone."

"Heat-stroke, asphyxiation, and heart failure," said Mercer.

Prescott nodded. "Mrs. Mathewson's story might not agree with yours, and while I realize that she will not be returning to Earth, it could be awkward if—"

"She wants to forget about it and so do I," said Mercer firmly. "That was my professional advice as well. There is also the fact that the media, if they got their hands on it, would be sure to imply all sorts of things which did not in fact happen. You see, both men were in such a mess that I don't *know,* from my very brief observation of their bodies, who killed who. It is possible, although not likely, that Stone made a comeback after Mrs. Mathewson was knocked out, so even she can't be sure. Then there are the possible effects on the boy of reading that sort of stuff about his mother, or finding out about it in later life. She won't talk about it, you can be sure of that."

Prescott looked relieved, but not completely. He said, "That's good. I told Mrs. Kirk about her husband on the way in—I said that his death was due to his being overweight combined with the heat and low oxygen content of the air. She could suffer, too, if it got out that he died fighting over a woman. But I'm more concerned about you, Mercer, and what you may say when we get back. We are all going to be heroes, you especially, and you could earn a lot of money from the media simply by telling the truth as you know it.

"I couldn't really blame you for doing that," he ended, "especially as you only wanted space experience to land a good research job on Station Three—"

"If you don't mind," said Mercer, "I would like a little more space experience—of a less dramatic nature, of course. And in any case, I am more interested in a job on Ganymede Base now. I don't want to embarrass the Mathewsons, or Mrs. Kirk, so if I can stay with the ship and toe the company line during the enquiry—"

"I'll be Captain," said Prescott.

"You almost dissuade me."

"I wasn't trying to do that," said Prescott quietly, "just trying to give you fair warning that I am a consistently nasty person who is unlikely to change anything but his uniform."

"*Neilson. We'll be ready to go in three minutes, Mercer.*"

As he turned to go, Mercer wondered if he would change very much. He was thinking of a very young boy who had played spaceman for two long and dangerous weeks, and of his mother, who would soon have him with her again. He had helped to save both of their lives and was beginning to feel responsible for them in an oddly possessive way, and the voyage was less than three weeks gone. It was a silly question, because he had changed in many ways already.

Exciting
Space Adventure
from
DEL REY